ADVANCE PRAISE FOR *GOODNIGHT, LADIES*

I love these Ladies, and I thanked every chapter of this novella for its intelligence, its dry wit, its dilemmas and victories, and for beautiful sentences that shine without preening. Truly, a pleasure.

— Elinor Lipman, author of *The Inn at Lake Devine*

Warm, witty, and wise. The overlapping stories of three women — three intelligent human beings — confronting, each in her own way, the inexorable approach of old age. I love this book.

— Nahma Sandrow, librettist, *Enemies, A Love Story*

I'm fascinated by the issues of age and solitude, which Zane Kotker deals with in a very appealing way — *Goodnight, Ladies* had me laughing out loud. Terrific writing, and the best, most unforced insights about age.

— Anthony Giardina, author of *Norumbega Park*

A haunting novella of linked stories, *Goodnight Ladies* illuminates the anguish of aging, the solace of memories, and the harrowing business of living alone. Her characters are spot-on believable and full of a just-bearable pathos.

— Anita Shreve, author of *Stella Bain*

Zane Kotker's ladies meet their goodnight with sparkle. Her fiction is a splash of fresh water.

— Rose Moss, author of *The Family Reunion*

Celebrated actresses "of a certain age" complain there are no good roles for them. Well, here they are — the ladies of *Goodnight, Ladies*. They're smart, funny, despairing, brave, reflective. . . . Read the book. The movie can't be far behind.

— Susan Yankowitz, playwright, *Night Sky*

Goodnight, Ladies

ALSO BY ZANE KOTKER

The Inner Sea
Try to Remember
White Rising
A Certain Man
Bodies in Motion

Goodnight, Ladies

A NOVELLA

Zane Kotker

Off the Common Books

2016

For dear friends all
living & dead
lost & found

CONTENTS

Chessa Gets a Dog
Nikki Counts the Minutes
Pru's Number Comes Up

❧

Chessa Meets a Poet
Nikki Lands on Marvin Gardens
Pru Pulls the Cord

❧

Where's Nikki?
What's Wrong with Chessa?
Why Is Pru Still Lying on the Floor?

Chessa Gets a Dog

On her twentieth birthday Chessa's first true love telephoned her during Christmas break to say that she was the one for him forever, but by the time she got back east he was dating a Wellesley girl. On her thirtieth she debated whether she should get divorced or pregnant. For her fortieth her husband, the second one, gave her a surprise party that temporarily rocked her sense of reality — coming into a dark room, a blaze of light, and there stood all her friends and family and Emily in her lion pajamas. For her fiftieth the three of them flew to Puerto Escondido to walk the white sands and only she got sick from brushing her teeth with local water. On her sixtieth George lay in a hospital bed recovering from heart surgery and she took him the most spectacular bunch of birds of paradise in a great glass vase. On her seventieth she quit the Unitarian Society, dropped her subscription to *The New York Times,* and got a dog.

She named him Jack J. Johnson. That was her first true love's name. It came to mind the instant she saw the dog's quick-moving nervous body in the pen at the animal shelter. The name made her smile. Now that George was dead and Emily approaching her forties, she felt curiously disconnected from them and more like her earlier self, the self before those two. Come on, Jack, she said with satisfaction, I'm taking you home.

The shelter worker advised her to tie the dog in the back of the station wagon: It seemed he had a history of rebellion. And he did whimper alarmingly on the ride over rutted roads toward the town's northern edge. Nor did he quiet when they reached the lone ranch house set on what had been farmland but which now sprouted a couple of trophy houses on one side and a row of mobile homes on the other. She stopped the car, opened the door. You can get out, she said, keeping hold of the rope.

They went inside to the kitchen, somewhat dim at noon when the sun was kept out by the hickory trees behind the house. This will be your bowl, she said, as she ran water into an old ceramic mixing bowl with the start of a crack in it. Come on, she said, settling the bowl in a corner of the kitchen by the radiator. It's yours. All I have is yours.

He was an edgy dog, uneasy, worried almost. How had he been living? Found near the college — the woman at the shelter had told her — no collar. He's had his shots, the shelter woman said; just rub the anti-flea cream into the skin on the back of his neck every month till winter and he won't need a flea collar. In the kitchen now, the dog approached the water, eyeing her. Go ahead, she said. It's only water.

He drank.

Had he been mistreated? It didn't seem so. He didn't flinch when she raised an arm or when she extended her hand to him. He smelled her fingers but didn't lick. The onions? She'd made cucumber pickles that morning. Okay, Jack, she said, let's look around.

She took him into the windowed sunroom on the west side of the house where soon a splash of yellow light would touch the couch and the rockers and the easy chair that had been George's favorite. He'd died in it, peacefully, or so she hoped. When he hadn't responded to her call to dinner, she'd found him here, permanently stilled, without a struggle, or so it appeared. The dog sniffed the easy chair and climbed into it. Very good, Jack, she said, very good.

Jack J. Johnson, the man, had fared well enough — she saw him now and then on the endless pundit shows. He'd become a forensic lawyer who was frequently asked for his opinion about the lack or presence of potential evidence in trendy cases. He'd married several times — two, three? — the marriages ending in what impasses the alumni magazine refused to note. How she'd suffered when he'd dumped her! Life for a while had become something you do anyway. Then she forgot him. And soon enough, none of it mattered.

This is better than death, she said to the dog, innit? Her daughter had spent some time in London and liked to break into Thames talk without warning. We go on then, she said to the dog. Was it students who dumped ya? Came to the end of the school year, did they? Or maybe you had a family? Yes, a family. And then a baby came and you were too nervous to be around a baby. Innit?

The dog went to sleep.

In the kitchen she made a spinach and avocado salad, covering it sparingly with a low-fat salad dressing she'd found in *Simple Things*. Her husband had maintained a cholesterol count of 184, while hers had soared to 277. Now she watched herself. There'd be no one here to find *her* dead in a chair. Maybe she'd better get one of those medallions to hang around her neck? Carrying her salad into the sunroom, she found a seat on the couch next to one of the Navaho rugs she'd bought when at her poorest, her motto being *pleasures before necessities*. The sun reached the dog's rump. He opened his eyes, shut them.

In the afternoon she looked up dogs on the Internet and decided maybe he was a mix of border collie and some sort of spaniel. Then she pressed a button on the keyboard that she hadn't meant to and the whole screen went dark. Her daughter telephoned. Some sort of event at her office, the stock market falling another notch, people being laid off. Emily herself didn't seem bothered.

"I'm okay for a while, Mom. What's up with you?"

"I got a dog."

"Oh, what's its name?"

"Jack. Jack J. Johnson."

"Funny name for a dog."

"That was my boyfriend in college."

"Oh."

She laughed. No responding laughter from her daughter.

"Why are you calling him that?"

"I don't know. It just came to me." She laughed again. Maybe her daughter was laughing? Sometimes it was hard to tell.

In the garden, she pulled up carrots and a bit of lettuce. She weeded the perennial beds, the yarrow so like minuscule broccoli, the ginger dark and glossy. No trips this winter, no skiing up in Canada, if Emily was right. Her growth stocks would be withering. Just as well, the slopes were crowded with snowboarders now. You could get killed. No beaches off Georgia, either. That's all right. She couldn't go anywhere anyway, not now, not with a dog. The dog would tie her down. That's why she'd waited so long. Now she had one.

She worked in the garden while the dog stood in the kitchen watching her from behind the screen door — his bark a rough sort of *ruff*. She would never have chosen a dog that yipped. She stood up, slowly, because you do get stiff kneeling, especially if you're tall. She walked up the flagstone steps to the kitchen, opened the door. Come on out, Jack. It's your yard.

He burst past her and ran into the garden. He pissed here and there and made for the woods beyond the hickories. She sat down on the warm stones of the back stoop. He'd come back. And if he didn't, she wouldn't suffer about it. If he didn't, she'd go skiing one last time despite the falling stocks. Yes, she would. Or down to that island off Georgia, maybe, when the snows came. No moping. Move on.

At dusk the dog returned and she fixed a bowl of Cheerios for him, along with some pieces of last night's chicken without the bones. Her fingers were greasy and she washed them under the faucet. It's good to see ya, she said as the dog ate, although she knew she would have been fine if he had not returned. She might have felt a little uncomfortable at first, responsible for locating him, making sure he was all right. Still, if he hadn't shown up in a day or two that would have been that. No dog. She was not someone to hold onto the past.

In the sunroom, she sat on the couch again and picked up "Pompey" from *Plutarch's Lives* of the Romans. Not that she was a thinker. She was a doer. But at book club Nikki had said it was time for them all to do a Golden Age reread and that way they could begin to clear their bookshelves against the time when they might have to strip down for assisted living. Chessa was already up to *P* in her reread, way ahead of everybody else. Of course she'd sold off most of George's books not long after he'd died, keeping only a single shelf in the sunroom. And now she was surprised at how vivid and colorful these little biographies of Plutarch's were. Not boring at all, even though they were from the past. They brought the world of 2000 years ago right into your lap. And made it seem like today. Nero reminded her a whole lot of George W. Bush. Pompey, it turned out, had as much money as Bill Gates and financed the wars of that time. She read a few pages, not many, and when Pompey entered Jerusalem, she shut the book.

Come on, Jack, she said to the dog. You get another shot at the wide-open spaces. She reached for the kitchen door. Out you go, one last time before bed. She stood in the kitchen doorway while the dog relieved himself. When he was done, he headed toward the woods and vanished. She stood there for a few minutes, keeping the screen shut against mosquitoes.

When he didn't come back, she went upstairs and got into her pajamas. Don't worry. He knows who fills his bowl. Give him some leeway. Let him run. Don't fence him in. How much is that doggy in the window? She brushed her teeth; she loosened the faded braid that ran a few inches down her back; she turned down her quilt. The lights from the mobile homes had come on; she knew there were couples over there, sitting out on their patio extensions, drinks in hand, imagining their futures together. Well, she was having *her* future with a dog.

Barefoot, she made her way downstairs. Her calcium pill, her coated baby aspirin, a half glass of water. The dog hadn't come back, wasn't standing outside the door, panting, waiting for reentry. She opened the screen door and stepped out onto the flagstones, letting the screen shut itself slowly behind her. She stood on the still-warm stones in the dark. She looked around, nothing out there. The trophy houses on the hill had gone dark. The woods, too, and motionless.

"Jack! Jack!" She called into the night, her throat closing on the words. There was a rustling in the woods but the dog did not appear. With her hand at her throat, she called again, louder, so much louder. "Jack! Jack J. Johnson, you come back here!" And she didn't like the sound of her voice.

Nikki Counts the Minutes

7:06

Waking, Nikki finds her brain redoing an old line of A. E. Housman's, *Now of my three score years and ten, /* seventy *will not come again.* It makes her smile. People think she's sixty. She feels fifty. But she's seventy and time is short. Every minute must count. Every minute must be golden. Ten years left? Fifteen? So few! She's solved that threat by simple multiplication, dropping the years to days, to hours, and finally to minutes, millions of them. Now, what to do with a cosmic phone card of unspent millions? Replace a lost pair of shears? Shop for grapefruit? Don't be ridiculous. It's serious — a tough job, turning hay into gold. She swings her legs to the cold floor and gets out of bed.

7:31

Naked after her shower, she flips her fingers through her short, Sassoon-reminiscent haircut and thinks of Karen, who some decades before came east with a travel kit containing heatable rollers. Beautiful Karen — her movie options, her style, her sensuality in cooking. Teach me, Nikki had said, on one of Karen's visits as they stood at the stove drinking wine and eating olives, stirring things. You have to *taste* it, Karen kept saying, *taste* it, don't just *think* about it. They drank too much, and Larry, eyeing them, suggested they not open another bottle. Now Karen's out there on the Pacific Rim in her house over the San Andreas Fault being cared for by a disconsolate Hal. "How is it?" She'd asked Hal the last time she telephoned. "It is," he'd replied in four slow syllables, "un-bear-a-ble." Karen had picked up on an extension to announce, and not for the first time, the birth of her grandchild. "What's her name?" Nikki had asked, unable to resist testing Karen. "Honey?" Karen had called from room to room in her California house. "What's her name, honey? Our granddaughter's name?"

She dries her glistening body and her first lover appears in memory, naked in a tenement tub. She had attended his funeral; friends read from his poems and one poem was clearly about her. He must have written it that night after their last fight. Cancer, buried in Queens. And cancer for Larry, too, good Larry, buried over at Brightside.

She creams her face and her hands that are so like her mother's. "Your mother has beautiful hands," her father said one summer night on a porch by a lake. "That's why I married her." A strange remark, opening the world of sexuality so gently. They were such good people. She bears them in her body, carries them in her genes, and wants so much to send them off into grandchildren. Stepping out of the bathroom, she takes them into the world.

7:49

One glance out her kitchen window and she sees before her the very thing she struggled to escape as a teenager: a leafy middle-class street in a pleasant New England town. Grown up, she has come to like her street. She even likes her solid brick house, is glad to retreat into its interior, to look out its windows at the cleverness of deciduous trees. They know what to do in winter — flee to the roots.

7:53

Oatmeal, raisins, walnuts, some bits of ginger, all hot from the micro. She picks up last night's magazine pressed open to an article on the long tidal river that runs through town, the river that bisects New England. The article explains what will happen to her valley in the next thirty or forty years as the planet warms. Winters will be milder, less snow will fall, pollution will increase in tributaries and in the river itself. The hotter summer will bring drier soil that will quickly absorb the runoff, causing the great river itself to shrink to a quarter of its volume. Increasingly intense summer storms will wash more sediment and pollution into the weakened streams. Some species that live in the watershed will be wiped out.

Humans?

The warming is the only thing that resigns her to not having grandchildren.

8:19

She rinses her cereal bowl and looks for her calendar, a tool as essential as her clock. People's Pantry at two. Christmas concert at four. She's careful to make a day plan because, without one, she might stare straight into time as it passes. Until now she was always struggling for more of it, juggling husband, children, her job at the library's First Call desk. Now, with time looping and sagging around her, she cannot remember what she wanted more of it *for*. As she sits with her morning coffee the most delicious lethargy comes over her. It begins somewhere on the right side of her head. She raises her coffee cup to the spot. The cup is hot against her palm and against her temple. Maybe it's the beginning of a stroke? She sits there and sees herself at the bottom of a grave stretched out in her winter coat. People are shoveling dirt on her. It lands on her lapels.

8:27

As she writes out her shopping list, the shortness of future blows in her face and behind her, too — a great wind rustling toward her buttocks. *What do you want to do with these last minutes?* I want. I want. More time? Not exactly. I want this time well spent. But how?

9:10

At the front door she hesitates. Lately she doesn't like to leave her house. Since Larry died, she's become more and more attached to these four walls, her house has become a person. In fact, it's her Significant Other. Her lover. She glances back into the high-ceilinged living room, at Larry's woodstove standing on its slate tiles, along the length of her Swedish kilim, to the bookcase where her parents' clock ticks. The clock presents a face to her, its hands move in recognition of her. The clock is alive. She and the house are one; its walls are her skin. I'll be back, she whispers. Just going shopping.

9:15

She avoids the icy spots in the driveway and reaches her garage without a fall. A few months ago, her old car burst into the smoke of an electrical fire. That's the closest a car can come to having a stroke. For a few days she considered living without a car, reducing her carbon footprint. But groceries? How to bring them home? For the first time she, not Larry, went to the used car place they'd trusted and bought a car, a white car. White as chalk. White as marshmallows. They said it would last twelve years. She'd be eighty-two, though she didn't mention this at the car place. She handed over thirteen thousand dollars. With that much money, Larry and she had made the deposit that secured the mortgage on their entire house.

9:21

Stopped at a red light, she can see past the new medical complex and on down the street to the Richardson-style library where she worked for seventeen years, bringing people together. She found widows willing to take in teenaged mothers, lawn jobs for newly arrived Cambodians, secondhand cars for boys who worked at MacDonald's. Then library funds withered, retirement packages appeared, and she took the bait. After all, Larry was about to retire. They could travel. Now Larry's gone, and she has her retirement money in low-risk funds. Thankfully, it's enough to live on. For what? Were she to appear at the library's First Call desk asking for help — Widow Seeks New Life — her former self would have known where to call, what to do. Her new self does not.

9:36

The recently built Super Super is so big that she runs the length of a couple of aisles to cut her shopping time. It's good exercise, with no fear of ice. Other people's carts are piled with whole chickens, legs of lamb, shoulders of ham, with six-packs of soft drinks, bags full of still-moving lobsters, green leaf, red leaf, potato chips, giant cartons of ice cream. Her cart contains a small pre-roasted chicken, one melon on sale, one red pepper, one brown pear, and a single pink grapefruit. She isn't doing her part for America. She passes a man with those little flags on his cart, the kind that go on the graves of veterans from World War II, Korea, Vietnam, Storm, Shield. She tries to hold her breath on the nights when Jim Lehrer shows those beautiful dead twenty-year-olds, silently, one by one. Not to take a breath, that's her tribute to them. She did march in one peace parade, the one before the invasion. Now it's too late. All her president wants her to do is buy the bargain paper towels. And the twenty-four-pack of toilet paper. These fill up her cart. Her cart doesn't look so forlorn anymore. Now she's saving America.

10:17

The clerk at the checkout looks Indian from India; the elderly bagger seems only to hail from the land of trouble; the woman in front of her speaks Spanish; the two Asian women behind her raise high voices in what language? She cannot tell Cantonese from Mandarin. She scans the immediate area. There are no other WASPS in sight. Her ethnic has floundered and run to ground. She's the enemy. Yet her WASP isn't the world's WASP. The world's WASP lives in Connecticut with a pool and a wet bar. Her WASP drinks iced tea, works hard, has never heard of the Rapture, tries to participate in democracy, and believes that the good might outweigh the bad if you would simply try again. What's so bad about that?

10:21

She sees *them* waiting for pickup, the eighty-year-old widows. They're sitting by the vending machines in a corner of the supermarket with their bags of groceries and their sparse, carefully arranged hair. Not talking to each other. Waiting for their van, for pickup and delivery back to the condos at the Farmingdale Community. Her friend Pru lives at Farmingdale, but not in the condos, she has a townhouse. She herself never wants to live segregated by age. They look impatient, these women. Do they not have cars? Or is it licenses? Their eyes not good? Maybe they've had an accident. More likely, they can't afford their car insurance. She hurries by. She has a car. She herself directs where she goes and when. She isn't sitting and waiting as if she were stuck in a tour group while someone in search of a lost sweater is holding up the bus to the Matterhorn.

She speeds past them, careful to keep her gaze straight ahead.

10:48

"This way, young lady," the gentleman shoe clerk says. Last week her dentist called her young lady for the first time. *This will pinch a bit, young lady.* She nearly ripped off her bib. She stands before an array of boots, furred, rubberized, high-heeled. She picks out a low-heeled pair and sits. The clerk straddles his footstool, pulls a tall black boot from a tissued box, unzips it, waits. She takes off her all-terrain shoes, extends a slender foot in its black tights. "Nice foot," he says. In the mirror she sees a quite attractive woman who doesn't look all that old — except for the greying hair, of course, and the pouches under her eyes and the lines when she smiles, if she smiles. The clerk zips her into the boot, concludes a now-so-rare flirtation with "No bunions!"

11:14

Carrying groceries over the ice, she makes it to her back door and the small hall virtually blocked by her older son's stuff: six big cardboard boxes and a wobbly wicker trunk. She herself has filled those boxes with her son's childhood papers and mementos. He doesn't get around to them. He doesn't sort them. He doesn't want them. They've been here for two years. Well, he does live in Seattle. With a wife who can't have children. Whenever they visit, Nikki's so glad to see him she forgets about the boxes. It wouldn't take him long. Just to sort through. Throw most of it out. Get it down to one box. She'd be glad to keep one box. When she does mention this to him over the phone, he tells her to throw it all out. She can't bear to do that. They are his childhood. She wants him to want these things. He doesn't want them.

She could, of course, move his boxes down into the cellar. But they're too heavy for her. And the cellar is already a mess: dust, wanton asbestos, and occasional dampness drape themselves over her seven years of tax returns, a rusted bicycle, the boys' vast stash of Legos. If the past is in the cellar, the future must be in the attic. Nothing there. She's cleaned that out, except for the papers, the melancholy journals she used to keep as her bright life went by. No time for that now. She puts the last grocery bag down on the kitchen table. Which bag has the rotisserie chicken in it?

12:19

The Wicked Widow's Cookbook for Those Who Don't Care

Chicken Leg

PREPARATION: Buy a rotisserie chicken. Don't bother unpacking the groceries; just find the chicken, pull off a leg, eat with salt and pepper.

GOURMET OPTION: cranberry relish

BETTER LIVING OPTION: napkin

HEALTH TIP: At the next meal, eat only greens.

FOOD FOR THOUGHT: A bird in hand is better than not.

12:23

As she eats her chicken, the college radio station discusses the economy. *The government is cooking the books!* says a man in urgent tones. *We're actually bankrupt and printing more and more money with no backing at all! The dollar is falling. Inflation comes when the dollar drops. Foreigners will stop buying our debt from us. Then we'll be stuck. We won't be able to pay off our own debt.* Larry's description of how the world works would be this: If a guy has no oranges, he wants other people's oranges. If a guy *has* oranges, he gets a gun to protect them from the people who don't have them.

Domestic oil production peaked in 1971! Where we used to have gushers, we now have deeper-lying oil fields, and that means pumping it out at a greater cost. We already import two-thirds of the twenty-one million barrels we use per day. This requires international entanglements and wars! Soon we'll be fighting for water, as well as oil. The Boomers are already filing for benefits. My advice? You've got a year or two to turn your lawn into a garden. To get your assets out of the market. To buy gold and silver. To stock your cellar with consumables.

How can she stock her cellar unless Nick goes through his boxes? She turns the dial on the radio. *It's a good day on Wall Street,* another voice assures her, *the market is in an upsurge.*

12:59

She crumples the paper towel she has used as a plate, tosses it smooth and easy into the wastebasket. Some of her friends don't know what to do with the time that's left them, either. Study Islam? Install LED lightbulbs? Give up their cars? Get a full body scan? Buy long-term health insurance — so obviously a racket? Pay out of pocket for a shingles shot? They settle on travel, film, plays, museums, the symphony, lectures. They eat culture. She doesn't want to eat culture. Doesn't want to stride forward through a cloud of it, swallowing culture, digesting culture, farting culture, shitting culture. She wants to pat dogs and look at the sparkle of sun on water. On the other hand, she wouldn't want to have to walk a dog three times a day. Maybe what she really wants is just to see again the round young faces of her boys — Nick the talkative, Matt the quiet — serious over their Legos, just as they used to be when she got home from the library in winter's dusk. No, that's not it. They're men now. Maybe what she really wants is just to be useful again.

1:21

The mail: two bills, three pleas for cash, a mailer from *The Teaching Company,* and a real letter. It's from the state university. Maybe they're giving her a prize? She has won prizes before, for volunteering.

It's a form letter. They're inviting her to join a program to test the flexibility of aging muscles.

1:47

The People's Pantry is located in a drafty building, so she leaves her coat on as she walks through the room of tables holding fresh apples, potatoes, squashes, turnips — all of which most of the clients ignore. They prefer canned food.

"Nikki Nickerson." She reminds the cheerful supervisor of her identity, eschewing as always the Caroline her parents had chosen for her.

"Wow," he says, "you're the third volunteer today. That's great!" It isn't great. It's crowded. He sends the red-haired girl behind the shelves to load the bonus bags for customers with kids. The volunteer in the plaid shirt is named Mark, and he claims one of the two weighing scales. Nikki takes the other. The supervisor reminds them that their clients are embarrassed at taking charity and should be greeted warmly and offered choices. Choices will give them a sense of power. He turns to the room, calls out, "Number One! Number Two!"

"Hello, Henry!" Nikki says to the whiskered man who is missing some teeth and who seldom talks. "Eggs or milk, Henry?" He nods and points, utters single syllables. "Tomato soup or corn stew?" She works through the list, dispatches him to the table laden with baked goods and breads, from which he chooses a crushed apple pie and a twelve-pack of donuts. "Good to see you, Henry," she says, as she weighs out his box at twenty-one pounds.

"Hi, Grace," she says to a blond woman, family of four. Grace wants pasta but only if there's plain tomato sauce to go with it. Chili but only if it's plain chili. "No plain chili, Grace. Just the kind with hot dogs in it." Grace knuckles under, accepts the hot dogs. That's all Grace is getting of power today.

Next comes a big man who speaks in an angry monotone, demanding this, pointing at that. Then a Hispanic woman whose daughter translates. The woman wants milk, but how much milk is granted for a family of six? Nikki turns to the quantity chart on the wall, pulls down her glasses, scans it unsuccessfully. "I'm slow," she apologizes to the daughter. "That's okay," the daughter replies. "Take your time."

Number Sixteen is a young man with matted hair, wilted shirt, and a blanket instead of a coat. He doesn't want powdered soup because he has no hot water. He doesn't want tuna because he has no can opener. She searches for ideas among the shelves: Ah! Beef soup in a paper carton, just add cold water. But no. He's a vegetarian. He finally accepts a couple of boxes of eight-grain cereal and a health candy bar. When he reaches the bread table, he stops moving. He stands there. He seems to be paying attention to something in the air around him. Is he seeing things? Does he hear voices? Finally, he picks up some whole grain rolls. "Thanks a lot," he says. "You've been very patient and resourceful." She thinks of the mother who raised this boy so well. If only she could call his mother, say, "It's okay. You can relax a little today. He's alive."

Number Thirty-One looks to be about thirty-one with a

daughter of about nine, both neatly dressed. Their hair is not stringy; they have all their teeth; their breath is good. The young mother chooses the health cereal and declines tuna, explaining, "Too much mercury." A baguette, a carrot cake. On the treat shelf Number Thirty-One spots a bag of coffee. "Is that beans or ground?" she asks. Then "Thanks, anyway. My grinder's broken." This pair Nikki wants to take home with her, then chastises herself for not also wanting to take the silent, toothless Henry.

An obese woman arrives a minute before closing. "Oat Bran or Special K?" Nikki asks, trying to shape a life toward health. "Oh, no, just give me the Sugar Pops." As the sweetest and fattest of foods fill the box on the counter, the obese woman lights up. Her delight is contagious. The other two volunteers, idle now, happily join in serving this woman. The red-haired girl asks, "Did you see the donuts?" Mark in the plaid shirt says, "There are custards in the fridge!" With an almost sexual excitement, the three of them pile on breads, pies, donuts, custards. Here is something they can do to better the world, to bring on happiness. From the treat shelf, the obese woman selects a prominent box of sugar and starts to leave, when the three volunteers, whispering among themselves, call out, "Wait, Wait!" The red-haired girl secures an abandoned birthday cake — *Happy 12th Birthday, Harold* — and settles it on top of the sixty-pound box.

"Nice work," the supervisor applauds them.

4:11

Carrying candles, the college singers file to the front of the holly-draped church — young women in black clothes with red scarves, young men in black jackets with red handkerchiefs in their pockets. The conductor raises her right arm: *Gaudeamus Omnes in Domino* they sing, from the very early seventeenth century. The King James Bible is still being translated. The English ships bringing dissenters from the Church of England to the tall-treed shores on this side of the Atlantic haven't left Plymouth or Bristol yet. Here where the white-steepled church stands, a tribe of long-faced farmers and fishers lived; they worshipped two gods — the god of order and the god of chance; in Jehovah of the Bible, the two forces merge.

Sopranos, altos, tenors, basses. *When David Heard that Absalom was Slain* they sing so plaintively, these young women who have not yet borne a child, these young men who have not yet tried to get their Absaloms to mow the lawn. *Would God I had died for thee,* they sing it in the abstract. They do not know the steps of the police on the front porch, the phone call from the college president, the e-mail from the war zone. *O Absalom, my son!*

If only she could feel the edge, just the edge, of what she'd known as a child — the sense that a great Creator loves her and the entire world. And, to set things right, He's turning Himself into a small baby and allowing Himself to be born on earth as His own Son and while He's down here, He'll see how we're all doing and show us The Way. Yet she can't recapture that sense. Does she actually want to? Only if it were true. But it isn't. It's man-made. It's anthropology. It's comparative religion. So why isn't that enough?

It is not enough.

6:21

From the freezer she takes a carton of carrot soup, decants it, sticks it in the micro. While it heats, she studies yet again the outline of Al Qaeda's master plan, clipped from a magazine — or was it a book? — and hung on her refrigerator by magnetic force.

Before you begin, study political science and everything else so
  you will govern well afterwards. Be ready with a full plan
  of allotting food and medical attention, courts and law.
  Get the United States to go to war with Iran. The Sunnis
  and the Shiites will join up together. Radical Islam will
  triumph. The sequence:

Phase 1, The Awakening, September 11, 2001

Phase 2, 2001–2006: Iraq becomes recruiting ground for

revolutionaries; Muslims donate money to replace what the USA takes or freezes.

Phase 3, 2007–2011: Focus on Syria and Turkey; begin to confront Israel.

Phase 4, 2012–2013: Arab regimes yield to radical Islam; attacks come against oil; USA overextends; electronic attack to destabilize USA economy; US dollar collapses; Islamic Caliphate declared.

Phase 5, 2014–2016: USA withdraws from Middle East; Israel a sitting duck; Islam allies with China; Europe falls apart.

Phase 6, 2017–2020, the Caliphate raises an Islamic Army, sons of Light fight against sons of Dark, Allah rules the world.

The microwave pings and she retrieves her carrot soup.

6:41

She wants to call up somebody and talk about life. She wants to say that she has realized no one will love her as the center of his life ever again. This desire to telephone and rattle on about life makes her wary. Usually it arrives on weekends or on those rare nights when she drinks too much. Tonight she hasn't been drinking at all. So? Call! Don't call! Now that no one else lives in the house, she argues with herself.

6:45

Risen to manhood, her younger son, the farmer, seems to look upon her as if she isn't entirely competent. Not the way he did as an adolescent — as if her very breathing could contaminate him. It's in a tender way now, touching her on top of the head, taking a light hold of her elbow as they cross the mud of his yard in Vermont. She dials his number. This one, Matt, never answers. *Leave a message at the tone.* Last time they spoke, she actually broke her silence and asked if he was planning to marry his Ellen, have kids. It's not like that anymore, Mom, he told her. Not like in your day.

No grandchildren? No small boy to bring Larry to life again? No small girl to bring her own mother back? Not to have grandchildren! It's unnatural, like a heart transplant. The tone sounds. "Hi," she says to whatever device was recording her. "Everything's fine. Nick and Traci will be coming in from Seattle around ten on Christmas Eve. Let me know when you two are coming down, okay?" She hangs up. To her kids, the cell phone is natural. It's nature.

6:48

Since she's gathered that she won't be having grandchildren, she's found herself drawn to the Neanderthals. They too went extinct. Of course, cutting world population in half could be the best thing for the species. Well, she's doing her part. The Great Voice in the Sky asks who will die for the species and somehow, without even telling her, her sons have stepped forward to volunteer, taking her with them out of the river of life.

7:18

She packs up several paperback books, lifts her parka from the hook in the mudroom, and steps out, snapping on the porch light so as not to return to a dark house. She gets into her car. At the corner she passes the Catholic church and then its parish house, the place where she took salsa lessons last year: thirty people moving their hips under a felt banner that showed Jesus's surprised face between two halves of a jaggedly split heart. "Give it more juice," urged the lithe little salsa teacher.

7:30

At the northern edge of town, light shines from the Cape-style house where Chessa lives above some mobile homes. There's only one other car in the driveway. She gets out, pulls her parka close around her, finds the front door unlocked, and steps into the entry hall. It's cold. Chessa keeps the house at sixty-two degrees and rents out a room to cover her heating oil. This allows her a bit of vacation money.

"Hey, Nikki! Come in!" With all the enthusiasm of the ski team captain she once was, Chessa bursts into the hall. "We're being stood."

A dog barks from some place of confinement upstairs.

Reluctantly, Nikki gives up her parka and then — rescue arrives. She's ushered into Chessa's living room, aglow with sparkling flames in the fireplace, with generously sized chairs equipped with black, red, and white pillows from Navaho crafters. And there's a bottle of wine and some chocolate chip cookies.

"Pru brought them," Chessa says.

And there's Pru, a plump woman occupying a substantial space on the couch. My name is not Prudence, she'd once informed her parents. It's Willow. Call me Willow. Her parents had not obliged. You learn such things in book club.

Embraced by this warm and colorful room, Nikki emerges from the shadowy palimpsest of a day spent with her own circling thoughts. "We're stood? Where is everybody?"

"Rachel called, sore throat," Chessa says. "Maxine's in the city. Sara's overwhelmed with Christmas. Tanya, well, you know Tanya. Abby had something, I forget what. And Dara's daughter went into early labor this morning. It's just us. You and me and Pru."

"Cozy, the widows three." Nikki sinks into the chair closest to the fire.

"Here's to you," Chessa says, pouring out half glasses of pinot grigio. None of them can drink the reds anymore.

All three raise their glasses in salute.

This is living.

They have been reading Jared Diamond's *Collapse: How Societies Choose to Fail or Succeed,* recommended by Nikki at the November meeting. Nikki always recommends books about world catastrophes. Chessa prefers any kind of self-improvement or a biography that runs from poverty to bounty. Pru tends to propose something more English and cheerful — a nice long novel about who inherits the house.

Now the fire crackles, the three women lean toward each other like so many Shakespearean witches, and Nikki begins. "He reminds me of Toynbee with his Golden Mean. Remember Toynbee?"

They do. They're the last of the old tradition, the old curriculum: Oberlin, Swarthmore, Mount Holyoke. They remember Tennyson and Lord Byron and the Peloponnesian Wars. They remember *amo, amas, amat, amamus, amatis, amant.* Nobody cares about Latin anymore, not even the beautiful architecture of it. *Hic, haec, hoc.* Time to toss this stuff out. That time has come. *That time of year thou mayest in me behold.* But they don't toss it. No, they don't. Because there are things a person is wise to hold onto. Things a person needs to carry close to the chest. Things that hold up walls, give structure to the contents of memory, allow you something to recite to yourself while having a root canal or receiving radiation. How they fear the

31

loss of such things. The loss of such things threatens a terrible time ahead, a loose, chaotic time, a time when anything could take the dative.

8:56

It was the absent Dara's turn to suggest what they read for January but Nikki has volunteered to fill in for her. She pulls the three paperbacks from her shoulder bag: Steven Pinker's *The Blank Slate: The Modern Denial of Human Nature;* Nicholas Wade's *Before the Dawn: Recovering the Lost History of Our Ancestors;* and Elizabeth Kolbert's *Field Notes from a Catastrophe: Man, Nature, and Climate Change.* Chessa and Pru vote for Kolbert because Nikki seems to like it best. The group doesn't read much fiction, though Pru often pleads for it. Like sex, fiction is private. The group reads to fix the world. It, too, hasn't much time left. It, too, doesn't seem to know what to do with these last few geological minutes before an unimaginable change.

9:00

The book discussion ends and Chessa gets up to separate the logs in her fireplace and calm the flames. They move out of the warmth of the fire and back to the chilly hallway. Upstairs, the dog barks again. Nikki zips her parka and Pru pushes her arms through her coat sleeves.

"My cousin fell on the ice last week," Pru says. "The doctor did a scan of her head. 'You're fine,' he tells her. 'The scan shows only that your brain has shrunk.' 'Shrunk?' my cousin asks. 'Yes,' says the doctor. 'As we age, the brain pulls inward from its outer limits. Don't worry. It's natural.'"

9:26

Driving home on almost-deserted streets, Nikki feels the pleasure of the last couple of hours begin to fade. Nothing really satisfies anymore. Everything fails, falls to the ground. Some gravity of age drains it away. Or is it because the things that happen to her these days don't register so deeply in the cortex as earlier things did? Maybe seventy years of memory takes all the space in your shrinking brain so that the new stuff can't sink in. Then she's home, pulling into her own driveway and here it is, the house that contains her, the place of self, the long familiar.

9:40

She's not tired but it's too late to get the stove in the living room going. Too heavy those pellets she'd have to carry up from the cellar. She sits on the couch wrapped in an afghan her mother made fifty years before. She picks up one of the novels sitting on the coffee table: William Golding's *The Inheritors*, published at about the time her mother set to work on the afghan. She's been weeding out her books and she's up to *G*. She doesn't open the Golding immediately. She doesn't want to go into another life — she wants so much for someone to come into hers. Not granted such a visit, she picks up the book and turns to page 1: *Lok was running as fast as he could.* Good, these are the Neanderthals with whom she now identifies. *His head was down and he carried his thorn bush horizontally for balance . . . .*

11:00

She channel surfs the news and has a little flash of dream in which she's a prisoner somewhere, some foreign place, not exactly Guantanamo, but somewhere quite uncomfortable and spare. She snaps off the TV and the living room light. She's alone in a dark room. This is good. She's reducing her carbon footprint; she's joined the war for world peace. She walks slowly, balancing on uneven floorboards. One day this couch, this afghan, will be here and she won't be. The boys will come and sort everything out at last. After that, just the windows and walls will remain.

And maybe Nick's boxes.

11:22

She puts paste on the toothbrush, regards herself in the glass, and brushes her teeth without looking in the mirror again. Should she grow her hair like Chessa's? Or let it go white, like Pru's?

11:30

Lying in bed with passing car lights on her wall, she suddenly knows what she wants. It's very clear. She wants something in the order of the Paleolithic human band. Shaggy-headed, roaming for food together. By now she'd be the group seer. She wouldn't have a car. Or car insurance. She'd read the stars in the sky for where the little group of twenty should camp and what seasons were coming up and how to treat sicknesses. People would honor her for it. She'd be a treasured resource. And if she had a toothache or a fever, she'd go to herself for the cure. She'd look out from under her furred forehead and say, "Honey, everything is going to be all right."

Pru's Number Comes Up

South of town rival orchards stood on opposing sides of a high ridge and beyond them the land opened to a great stretch of meadow and a view of hills, the last undeveloped prospect for miles around. Then gradually the road dipped into descent and soon a sign announced The Farmingdale Community for Independent Living, in gold letters against a green background. Roman letters, to be precise, followed by an italic promise: *Time to grow again.* Turning in, you passed a tranquil man-made pond surrounded by a stand of white birches barely budding in the March damp and by clusters of attached condos known to the community as Pondside. Beyond the condos, signs pointed left to Admin and straight ahead to Memory

Lane and right to The Hill, where groupings of townhouses, more generous and architecturally appealing than the condos, took their stand. In one of these townhouses Pru paced a red-tiled kitchen holding a land line phone to her ear as she listened to the voice of her daughter coming to her across the continent from the state where doctors help you die.

"But Mum ... you've been waiting for this for years and now you don't want it?"

"Well, you see, sweetie ... a move like this is kind of ... well, ominous."

"Ominous?" Cori's voice rose. This was Pru's emotional child, the other one was affect free. "But you *said* it was perfect."

"I know." Pru ran her plump, beringed hand over the granite of her countertops. Down in the condos the countertops were vinyl. "But now I'm not so sure."

"Okay, so don't go."

"But I'm finally number one. It took years to get to the top of the condo list and now I have to go ...."

"No, you don't!" Since she'd given up trying to survive in a traveling dance group and begun teaching, Cori had taken on a surprising authority. "You're a free agent, Mum. You can do what you want."

Pru's very words to her daughter from the age of Gloria Steinem, shot back to her like bullets: She tried a different tack. "Listen, sweetie, townhouse fees keep going up. Pretty soon I'll have trouble paying them."

"Okay. I get that. But you've been waiting for a place at Pondside ever since Dad died and now you don't want it. What am I missing?"

"As I said, this would be my last move! It's where I'd die."

"Come on, Mum. You're not dying! Don't say stuff like that!"

"I know I'm not dying. It's just that the place they're offering me . . . it's just got Last Stop written all over it."

"Well, it's not such a bad place to . . . well . . . I mean, anyway, don't people die in hospitals?"

Her thirty-five-year-old child, too young to get what age makes all too clear: It's really you. Not the whole human race and not sometime far away in the future. It's just you, a tiny spark going out, maybe tomorrow at noon or, less dramatically, at ten of two.

"You're right. They do. But most of the time they get the chest pain or feel the lump while they're in their own bedrooms or showers and that's the beginning of the end. Hey, never mind. Forget it. It's a great condo, 151. It's on a corner. I'll have windows on three sides. What am I complaining about?"

"Well, exactly! That's what I meant. It's perfect for you."

"Yes, it's just my size. Just the size for one old . . . uh, older woman who doesn't even *want* a cat." Oh god, now she was sounding like her own mother, a woman who had everything, including the belief that she was about to lose it all.

"Are you thinking of a cat again?"

"No, sorry. Just joking. How're you? Did you try that vegan cake recipe I sent you from the paper?"

If only Cyrus were alive. He'd know what was bothering her. He'd know what to say. He'd say, don't worry, my love. Pondside is fine. You'll still be you.

Pru stepped over the depression left in the cream-colored carpet by her husband's wheelchair and set the heavy tray down on the coffee table in front of the enormous couch that Cyrus had loved for its length.

"*You* know what I mean, Nikki," she said, taking a seat at the other end of the couch from her friend. "Once I'm out of the townhouses and down into the condos, that'll be it. No more turns in the road, just straight ahead to . . . ." She raised her soft palms to the void.

"I know." Nikki laughed. Just walking into Pru's townhouse she'd felt herself to be bent at the waist and shuffling, unable to prepare a Christmas dinner or understand a DVD player.

"I can't decide. It's killing me."

"Okay, try this." Nikki fell back upon her years at the First Call desk. "You said you needed money. If you move down to the condos, you'll have more money. You could travel, see the world."

"No matter where I went, I'd be coming home to Pondside. Those women don't do anything. They don't drive anywhere. They take the van wherever they go. A tenth of a mile to the post office and they take the van . . . ."

Nikki remembered her motto: First, listen.

"They change, they fall out of the world somehow." Pru raised the lid of the silver pot to check the color of the tea and filled the two waiting cups. "They watch a lot of television, they shrink to half their height and pop off. What's there to look forward to down there?"

"Assisted living?" Nikki offered. They both laughed.

Ample Pru leaned back against ampler pillows to say in a more mellow tone, "We were looking forward to so much when we moved up here. Our kids getting married. Grandchildren. We hardly noticed the condos. And god knows we tried not to look over the hill to Memory Lane. I mean, we were glad all that stuff was available. Just not for us. And, think of it, the things I'd have to get rid of! The living rooms at Pondside are so tiny. And there's just the one bedroom. How could I have an overnight guest?"

"Who's coming?"

Pru stiffened. "Well, Charlie told me he'd come up and help me move. *If* I move. You know, Nikki, the other thing is . . . up here I was a mother and a wife. Down there I'd just be another widow."

"Okay, I've got it," Nikki said. "You're far too young for Pondside. Wait till you're eighty. Trim your budget some other way. Sell your diamond. There's a month's fee right on your finger!"

Pru smiled. "You really think I'm too young?"

. . .

Dressed in a spring suit grown a bit tight, Pru sat in the Admin Office looking over a brass-knobbed desk at a young man sporting a pale blue tie. "I'm afraid that wouldn't work, Mrs. Wells," he was saying. "That's simply not part of Farmingdale policy."

"Why not?" Pru had been a girl pretty enough to charm both football captain and yearbook editor, and the sense of that power stayed in her bones. "Just put the number two person in this condo and next time there's a vacancy, I *promise* I'll take it." She smiled, as if a smile could still do the trick.

He shifted in his chair. "As I said, Mrs. Wells, I'm afraid that won't work. When you're number one on our waiting list, you have to take whatever comes up or go back down to number . . . ." He flipped open his computer. "One hundred and thirteen."

"I see. And by *comes up*, you mean that somebody has died, is that right?"

"You could put it that way, Mrs. Wells. But we don't."

"Of course you don't. And how much *turnover*, how often do things . . . *open up*? Just how long would it take for me to rise to the top again?"

He leaned back in his swivel chair. "Only the Good Lord Himself knows that, Mrs. Wells. But I would guess maybe seven years, eight."

Pru found her manners slipping so fast she could hardly catch hold of them. "Please, what's the date by which I have to decide?"

"Monday."

"So quick!"

"Mrs. Brandt's son has had her furniture sent up to his summer place in Maine. The cleaning women are in 151 as we speak."

"Removing all traces?"

"What did you say?"

"Nothing." Pru stood in her one-inch heels, wavered a bit, and pronounced a phrase Cyrus had so often employed though she herself had never used: "I'll get back to you."

On April Fool's Day Pru and her son walked down the hill to the condos. At the stone steps outside unit 151, Pru took a key from her pocket and said, not for the first time, "It's wonderful of you to come on such short notice, Charlie. Really wonderful. I didn't want to do this all alone. I really didn't." She pushed open the condo door. "Dad and I were so happy in the townhouses, before his stroke." She stepped into the empty foyer. "I hate leaving him behind up there, all by himself. Even if he's dead."

Charlie stepped in behind her and shut the door. She took a few steps, leading him into the unfurnished living room with its smell of cleaning fluids.

"Nice! Lots of light," said this ruddy man beside her, this man who had somehow metamorphosed from a towheaded fellow in shorts and sandals into a relaxed and competent middle-aged man.

"This is the last chance to see if we can find a way to fit my couch into this room before Mighty Movers gets here." The slightest of echoes held Pru's words in the air.

"Well, let's get at it," Charlie said. "How big's the couch?"

"Sixty-eight inches." Pru took a tape measure from her pocket and handed it to her son. She'd already measured the spaces herself, but it was so good to have Charlie do it. It made her feel that the whole family was moving down here with her.

He held the tape straight across the back of one living room wall. "Not here." He turned to a longer wall, and Pru studied him — his organized, sequential movements, warmed by how much he resembled her husband. Her husband who, for the first time in her adult life, would not see the place she called home.

"On a slant here might be okay," Charlie concluded. "Except a couple of inches of it would hang out into the hallway." He stood up, handed back the tape measure.

"Well, that's that." Pru had pretty much settled on this conclusion before Charlie arrived. "It will have to go to the Salvation Army. No more decisions now. We can go out to lunch. Unless there's something else you want. Your father's desk?"

"No, thanks, Mum. I took everything I wanted when you guys sold the house on Jefferson Street."

"What about for the girls? The little brass bed? The old doll cradle?"

"Oh, they've got everything, believe me. Stephie sees to that. Doesn't Cori want some things?"

"She says my stuff is 'a bit rococo'."

"What does that mean?"

She laughed. "I think it means she's got her own style."

"When's she coming east, anyway?" He headed toward the door and Pru followed.

"June, after school gets out." Saying that, Pru felt suddenly bereft. Once Cori came and saw her here, it would really be over, that part of her life, marriage, the townhouse, Cyrus.

"At least you'll be settled in by then."

"That's what . . . ." Her voice caught in her throat. "What I'm afraid of."

"What'd you say?" Charlie was already walking toward the door, already opening it.

She cleared her throat. "That's what I hear, dear. That's what they say. I'll be settled in by summer."

"Well, that's good, Mum."

He held the door for her and she walked out with no expression on her face, like a defendant who has lost his case, a man of whom the press next day reports "he showed no remorse."

Weeks of unpacking boxes, lining drawers with shelf paper, nodding at neighbors, and finally June came, bringing the long-awaited Cori. Pru heard the car and hurried to the door. But who was this young woman approaching? Not her hippie daughter with trailing hair and clothes. No, this was a woman in her prime: blond hair darkening to brown and cut in a new style that puffed out on top, real clothes that didn't seem to have been resurrected from the Salvation Army.

"Oh, sweetie," she said, embracing her daughter.

"Mum!" Released from embrace, Cori looked around. "Just like your townhouse! Only smaller."

"Cozy enough. And you, you look wonderful!"

"Thanks. But hey, I thought you hated venetian blinds."

"Mrs. Brandt's son left them. They're growing on me."

"Everything's so new!"

"Look at this." Pru lifted a rose-flowered pillow from a recently delivered chair and took hold of a loop. "You pull here and it turns into a bed. I reserved the Hospitality Room for you up at the Inn but now that this is here, you can give it a test run."

"Oh, Mum, thanks, but I was looking forward to the Hospitality Room. It's got that wide-screen TV."

Pru let go of the loop, replaced the pillow, and found that the two of them were standing somewhat awkwardly in each other's space.

"Come on," she said, moving toward the kitchen. "I've got the water on."

Cori made a quick survey of the avocado-tinted surround and pointed to a shiny object on top of the refrigerator. "That I remember, that brass bowl. Didn't it used to be on Dad's desk?"

"Yes. I had to get rid of his desk." Always a Daddy's girl, this daughter of hers. Pru turned her attention to the whistling teakettle. "There's hardly anything here left from the Jefferson Street house. And now not all that much from the townhouse, either."

"So it's okay here?" Cori leaned against a counter. "You weren't so crazy about this place in the spring, if I recall."

"Oh, that was silly of me. I don't know what I was thinking."

When Pru had all the fixings laid out on the big silver tray, she gave it to Cori to carry. Cori took it into the living room, set it on a small coffee table, and took a seat on her mother's pullout chair. "You don't miss the townhouses, then? You see your friends up there?"

"Oh, I haven't been up on the hill lately." Pru lowered herself into an old wing chair she'd had re-covered in a fabric replete with yellow flowers.

"You don't go up there?"

"No. That's somebody else's house now. A nice man. His wife died, so he moved here. Wes? Win? Something like that." Just for a minute, at closing day on the townhouse, she'd wanted to take his arm, to stay on up on the hill with him, to live that part of life over again.

"Mum?" Cori said. "Mum?"

"Oh, sorry. No, I don't go up there much. We have everything we need right down here. Couldn't be more convenient. I don't know what I was so worried about."

Cori sat back in the new chair. "So it's perfect, after all?"

"Yes, dear. It's perfect."

"But what about your old friends? What're they doing?"

"Oh, they're always flying around somewhere, visiting their families."

Cori held tight to her teacup and changed the subject. "Where's your friend Chessa?"

"She got a dog."

"That was last year."

"I guess so."

"And what about Nikki?"

"Haven't seen her lately. Still worrying about the world, I imagine."

"You sure you're all right, Mum?"

"What do you mean?" Pru put a hand to her hair. "Do I look funny?"

"Oh, no. You look fine. Fine."

"Well, now. That's how I am, sweetheart. I'm fine."

Pru reached for the teapot and suddenly her face felt so warm, as if she might be blushing. For a minute, she didn't quite know where or who she was. All familiarity had been sucked out of the room. Cori looked so strange with her hair swept off her forehead like that, older, and not necessarily the natural outcome of the white-blond child whose every feature was emblazoned in her mother's brain. When Pru picked up her tea, the cup rattled against its saucer.

Chessa Meets a Poet

Jack growled when the new renter first appeared at Chessa's door and that should have been a clue. This Natalie took over Emily's old bedroom and Chessa's kitchen as well, with every night the same fare — any tomato and cheese combination known to be palatable to humankind. At first, Chessa went along with it. It's good to hear a human voice at supper, innit?

No offense, Jack.

And at first it *was* okay. Natalie told stories of her work as a geriatric nurse to cloistered nuns down in Connecticut. "Some of those old girls, seventy, eighty, have the skin of twenty-year-olds. Never been out in the sun." Fortunately, Natalie was afraid of dogs and after the first month of eating in the kitchen with her renter, Chessa said, "You can have the kitchen, Natalie. I'll take the sunroom with Jack and get him out of your hair."

In the sunroom Chessa sat in George's chair with Jack beside her and considered husbands. The first had left her right after Emily was born. A note on the kitchen table: *Good-bye.* She'd plunged into that early marriage to escape everything she'd already known at home. Sometimes you just have to take action. How else can you get a taste of anything? If only her daughter would take a plunge now and then. But Emily hung on and on to things, wasting her best years with that dud of a software man. Something had to change.

Next day she got herself up to the cemetery for a little talk with George. "I'm going now," she told him, as she settled a pail of blue phlox by his grave. She listened for reply. She looked at the headstone she'd refused to share with him, even though it would have been a whole lot cheaper. She wanted her own stone. She was a person. A person in her own right. Wasn't that what that little weasel of a man who'd shot JFK — his mother, wasn't that what she'd said? No, what she'd said was "I am a mother in history." Well, good luck, honey. I'm a mother in theory, and I won't really know how I did as a mother in reality until Emily is content. I do know this: I couldn't have tried any harder. But George, listen. Emily's making herself a set of pottery dishes, sort of like a trousseau, don't you think? That's not what I came to say, though. I came to tell you that I need more than Natalie.

She stopped, listened again.

See? You don't even answer me! I know. You can't. It's not your fault. It's okay. But you see what I mean, don't you? I'm still walking around up here in the air and I need somebody who's upright. I'm no nun. Maybe it'll be an example. For Emily, I mean. If I find a man, maybe she'll find one, too. I just wanted to tell you, I'm going now. I didn't want it to come as a surprise and I promise to get buried here, right beside you.

With my own stone.

Back home she moved slowly about her kitchen, the dog at her heels waiting for life, love, and sustenance to fall to the floor. You were good, Jack, she assured him, still are. But you know what? You're just not enough. And believe you me, kid, we can't just wait around for things to happen. We have to up and do.

Seventy-two: But she lied about it when she created her Match. com profile, signing in as MountainLady from the couch in the sunroom where no one could see her. *Age 62, tall. I like all the things you like.* Then she got down to business, averaging out the men's profiles to find their favorite things: thunderstorms, fires in fireplaces, walks on the beach, eating out, dancing in the dark. She didn't bother winking at any of the men. She went straight to the next step, the e-mail note. Writing was her pleasure. She'd always been good at it. Nothing like sitting down from ten to maybe noon and entering a world you've made up for yourself. *Seeking warm, gentlemanly man, age sixty-two or less. Here's hoping he likes to hike and canoe cuz*

I'm an outdoor person. Companionship? Yes. Sex? Not right off. We have to be friends first. But if we rock, we rock. She couldn't believe she'd said that. But she's discovered that if you don't mention sex at all, you don't get any replies. And she wanted replies. Replies took up the afternoon. That left the evenings for television. She no longer read. Not after being on the computer so much of the day. TV was so relaxing. She could sit there in George's chair and fall asleep watching. That way, when she got into bed, she wouldn't need the sleeping pill. And she'd have the next day's e-mailing to look forward to.

Kayaking is my delight, she wrote, *nosing around on small rivers, looking into the water. How about you? Oh,* replied RiverboatMan, *I love those small rivers, too. They really turn me on. But personally, I prefer a canoe. Two can fit in a canoe. Can you canoe? Hah ha.* She didn't like old jokes. She wanted something a little more subtle. So she let Riverboat go and moved on to ProsperousPoet. Huh? There's prosperous and there's poet and the two don't mix. She knew that much. Even Walt Whitman was poor as a dog. Sorry, Jack, she said in his direction.

But hey, this may be the one. Prosperous had been a biology teacher for most of his life. That part was good. She liked biology. She liked poetry, not the gloomy kind you have to work at. *Have you published any of your poems?* she inquired. *I'd love to read one.* And there he was again! Replying immediately. It was almost like holding hands. *No, I don't send out my poems, sort of like Emily Dickinson, you know. But having looked into a microscope for decades, I feel I know what life is about. Survival and reproduction, I'm still surviving. (Reproduction? Sigh.) Love sailing. Have a boat. Want a woman.*

The man knew how to cut to the chase. Prosperous could be okay. And she needed someone with a little cash. *I watch Nature and Nova,* she wrote back, and went on for two pages about the Serengeti. She waited. If only he didn't tell her he liked *Two and a Half Men* the way FancyMan had. Sometimes she wished she hadn't had the old-style education she'd received; it separated her from a lot of perfectly nice men who got *who* and *whom* confused by day and watched *Two and a Half Men* at night. Wait! Here was Prosperous online again.

MountainLady, I need to meet you. I don't travel too easily. I wonder if you could join me for lunch down here in Connecticut. How about Wethersfield? We could meet at the Chinese restaurant on Route 5 in town. They have a good buffet. I feel you are perhaps the one for me. You ask about my life, my wives, you say, as if I had so many. Well the truth is, I have been married and divorced but only once. I have a darling daughter who put me on Match because she fears I'm lonely. And because she thinks I'm such a great guy. Who wouldn't love you? she asks me. It's hard to resist pep talks like that. I like what you say about walking on beaches and sitting by fires, and boats. And, as you know, I have one. As for thunderstorms, my god! They're just about my favorite thing. I was a religion major at Yale and thought of going into the ministry but duh! I lost my belief and that's it, the whole story. Your saying you worship rain and sun and the things of the garden, that really turns me on. Girl, I say to myself when I read your e-mails, I could really get close to you. So how about it?

Wethersfield, she replied, *I went to a wedding there once so at least I can find it. Please bring a poem. I myself do crocheting. Maybe I'll bring a pillow I did, but don't let the word pillow give you ideas! I don't, after all, call myself MountainWoman. It's Lady, MountainLady. What about a week from Friday at noon? I think I can make it then. Did I tell you I'm tall? I mean really tall?*

Noon, he wrote back, *the Chinese place. Did I tell you I'm short? I mean really short? My lips should about reach your breasts. Forgive me. That's premature. Actually, I used to be five ten. But I've shrunk.*

Red flag, the bit about the breasts. Danger sign. Should she drop him? But everything else sounded so good. Even five ten was okay, she'd been five eleven once. And she'd shrunk, too. Maybe he was just nervous. She hadn't yet made it past e-mails to a Match.com lunch and she wanted to see what one would be like. *Forgiven for the crude remark,* she wrote, *but barely. I'll be wearing a yellow jacket.*

Lady, I'll be wearing my heart on my sleeve.

"Promising," Nikki said after book club, "if a bit crude."

"You're crazy," Pru said. "You could get killed!"

. . .

It was a short drive, only an hour and a half, and Chessa got there early. Why was she doing this? She preferred the old days when men made the calls, paid the bills, and announced their intentions. When women kept saying no until they said yes. That was simple. This was not. ProsperousPoet could be anyone. Not a serial killer, or probably not. But who knew? Never mind, it was a public place, a busy street. Yes, there was the restaurant sign now, a block off. He'd said Yale, he'd gone to Yale, so how could he be all bad? Because maybe he hadn't gone to Yale. Because maybe he was a pathological liar. You can't know. You have to plunge in. You see, Emily? Parking in the public lot, she got out of the car and pulled her linen jacket close.

It was only ten of noon and she was getting nervous. Not physically scared; she'd been taller than all the boys in sixth grade and had never since worried about being overpowered. It scared her to hurt people's feelings, though, and of course she didn't like to get her own feelings hurt. Clearly this game was a setup for hurt. Still, what else was there? Every brick-and-mortar man she knew was married or gay or sick. Okay, here she was, a mere storefront away from the Chinese place. Slowing her steps, she paused in front of a nail salon. Twenty-five dollars to get your toenails painted? Good lord, she never spent money like that on things she could do herself. Quickening her steps, she walked right past the Chinese place, surreptitiously glancing in at disappointing plastic booths, an absence of tablecloths. She picked up her pace, kept walking on for two or three blocks more, waiting for noon to show on her cell phone before turning back to the restaurant. When it did, church bells tolled: No man is an island. It tolls for you, MountainLady. It tolls for you, ProsperousPoet.

It was fairly dark inside the restaurant and only one booth was occupied. At it sat a man studying the entrance door — Prosperous himself, no doubt, making his first appraisal of her. And she took hers of him: He is small. He is old. I kid you not.

"Don't get up," she said as she slid into the seat opposite him. She didn't want to view the entire man just yet.

"Looking good." He gave her a sort of smile.

"Thanks." She put her pocketbook down beside her. "Nice place. You come here often?"

"Once a month or so. I meet all my respondents here."

His respondents. She cleared her throat. "And how long have they been responding?"

"Two years."

"Two years! And you haven't found anyone yet?"

"Not till today. Sorry, premature again, though I assure you I'm never actually prema —"

She stopped him with a wave of the hand.

He laughed, said, "As you know from my e-mails, I do get carried away. Sorry, here's the story: I meet women whom I find interesting and they don't find me interesting. Or vice versa.

They like me and I don't like them. Or they like my boat or my English sheepdog and that's not what I'm about. I'm about my poetry, now that I've retired. A poem a day, keeps the blues away."

"Did you bring one?"

He laughed. "Did you bring your pillow?"

She laughed.

He smiled in a guilty way.

There *were* no poems, she realized.

"Come on," he said, "It's self serve." He stood. She stood. The top of his head came just below her shoulder. He looked older than her grandfather had at ninety-one. Did she look this old? She wasn't ready. Not for that.

At the hot table, she picked out the less wilted of the vegetable dishes and loaded up on egg rolls. He filled his plate to the edges. Still growing? Back they went to their booth, these two — hah ha — sixty-two-year-olds.

"Do you have children?" he asked. "Grown?"

"I have a daughter. She's living in Burlington. Vermont."

He nodded. "Married?"

"No. She'd like to be. Or rather, I'd like her to be."

"Not me," he said. "I like to keep things simple."

"Good idea." She meant that. She had no intention of remarrying. It could lead to complications, her daughter, his children, their marriages, their divorces. No telling where your mother's Persian rug would end up. Besides, she'd promised

George she'd show up in the ground beside him. Wait, was Prosperous telling her she'd flunked his test? How could *he* consider *her* not up to snuff?

He was smiling in a better way this time. So okay, she'd passed. Why did she care? He hadn't passed *her* test, after all. "You mentioned a daughter?" she said.

"I did. My Jenny. She's a doll. I've a son, too, but Norrie and I don't get on. I'm waiting for him to get to be a grown-up but so far — he's fifty-one — no dice."

There's the proof. He couldn't possibly be anywhere near sixty-two. "Did you have a falling out?"

"More like a falling apart. He did the drug thing and I blew up at him. I thought that would be good for him. It only set us apart, though. Now he's off to places unknown, Amsterdam, last I heard. He calls every couple of years."

"That must be terrible."

"It is."

Oh dear, she was starting to feel sorry for him. And already she knew she could never touch him. She was going to have to let him down. It wasn't going to be easy. She must be careful how she did this. She couldn't do it yet. They were still eating. She asked about how he spent his day and he went on about that at length, relieved to get off the topic of his son. She tried to find the golden part inside him. She did believe that everyone had a golden part.

When he went back to the buffet bar for seconds, she kept

to her seat and checked the time on her cell phone. Fifteen more minutes, bare minimum. Then, out.

Really, what was she doing here? Maybe she just needed to ditch Natalie and get a different renter, someone whose experience moved beyond nuns and cheeses. Yes, get rid of Natalie somehow, install a lonely, divorcing professor in, say, his sixties? Ten minutes to go. Maybe she could just bolt out now, while Prosperous was at the buffet table. Or vanish into the ladies room and crawl out the window, the way women did in movies from the 1940s. Outside, below the window, Clark Gable stood waiting to catch them.

He brought back a coconut pudding topped with ice cream and sweet cherries from a can. There was politics to talk about and art and what the world was coming to, and she did her best to make at least this quarter hour of his life a sweet one. And when the clock outside struck one, she'd done her part. It was time to go.

He summoned the waiter for the check.

"So," he said, leaning across the table, "what do you think?"

Coconspirator, she leaned forward too. "About what?"

"About us. Are we a number?"

"You know . . ." she stalled for whatever might come to her. What came was a lie. "You know, I went on another lunch earlier this week." Well, she did have FunlovingOrthodontist scheduled for the following week. "And it was quite enjoyable. We're planning to meet again in the near future. I didn't want to cancel this meeting of ours because I'd said I'd come. And here I am. And you. Here you are. But I think it would be wisest for me to say that I'm an old-fashioned person and would not want to be seeing two men at the same time, so I guess the answer is that I'm sorry. You're an interesting man, though I wish you'd brought a poem. But I think this is it. And thank you, thank you. You're a very nice man."

"That's what they all say." He was reaching for the check. He was studying it. He was in fact dividing the total in two. "Twelve for each of us. With a two-dollar tip for each, that'll be fourteen for you."

Modern times. She laid her bills on the table. She stood up. She put out her hand. He took it. He held it to his lips. "I'm a small man," he said, pulling on her hand, pulling her toward him, his face nearer and nearer to hers, "but I've got the biggest cock you've ever seen in your life."

She snatched her hand away and walked off backwards, holding her breath. He didn't move from the booth. At the door, she turned around and walked out, breathing freedom. She took a few steps and ducked into the nail salon, hurrying to the back, where he couldn't possibly see her from the street, couldn't possibly follow her. Ushered to a leather chair with a whirlpool in front of it, she sat. She took off her shoes and knee-highs. She rolled up her pant legs. She stuck her feet into the warm water.

"Divine," she said to the Asian man who reached to soap her heels in his soft, strong hands.

Nikki Lands on Marvin Gardens

Standing at the window of the brick house in town, Nikki watched the grand boy climb out of the camp van carrying a small violin case under one arm and something she couldn't determine under the other. She hadn't had the pleasure of such a visit for months. Once he was in her foyer she could see he'd changed from a delicate blond and hazel-eyed boy into something larger, something fueled for conquest. He was thicker, warier. Not testosterone. Not yet. He was only nine.

"You've grown," she said, instantly regretting the cliché.

"I guess," he said, following her into the spacious living room of the brick Georgian. "Isn't it funny, that everyone else can see when someone is taller except for the person?"

"Yes, it is," she assured him. "And it's funny how adults can tell kids they've grown, while kids aren't allowed to mention that adults look a bit older."

He laughed. That's what had endeared him to her. That and his thoughtful expression and the fact that she had no grandchildren. A grand boy would have to do. She'd fallen for this distantly related child the first time she'd seen him, sitting on his father's lap in a baby's stretch suit and fisting the keys of her piano with amazement at the sound he could produce.

She led him over the kilim to the far end of the room where afternoon sun slanted through filmy curtains. June, and it was hotter than usual — a heat that could mean global warming. You can't be certain. Elizabeth Kolbert didn't have any doubts, though. When she bent to clear the coffee table of magazines, the boy put down the violin and removed what turned out to be a Monopoly set from under his arm.

"I creamed my Dad," he told her, with a smile reminiscent of a couple of guys in the Pentagon with ties to Halliburton.

She'd planned to offer him the colorful labyrinth of Chinese Checkers or maybe some peaceful digging in the little herb garden she was tending out back or a nice walk down in the meadow. But never mind, Monopoly was fine. "How'd you do that?"

"He landed on Boardwalk with a hotel on it. Three thousand buckaroos."

"Three thousand bananas, you say?"

"Buckeroos."

"It's the same thing, where I come from. Let's play."

He used to ask her *How do you do this? How does this work?* Today, he gave instruction. "You be the banker. I'll handle the property."

She sat obediently doling out the paper bills in their different colors. The tawny one-hundreds reminded her of her brother. He'd always held a bunch of them close to the chest as he proceeded to roast her in game after game, until the one time she'd beaten him, after which he'd kicked the Monopoly board under the couch and never played again. She mustn't win this game. And she mustn't lose it on purpose, either. That would humiliate the boy. Her own grandfather had let her win at Chinese Checkers one terrible night and she'd had to save her pride by refusing the ice cream sundae.

"You go first." She handed over the dice.

He rolled and landed on a property in the board's cheap corridor. Using his fingers, he calculated the intricacies of purchase. He could handle adult nuance with wit but because his holistic school shunned rote learning, he couldn't add or subtract with any speed. Multiplication? What's that? She rolled, landed on Chance, paid a poor tax of fifteen dollars.

"I will crush you!" he said.

"Oh, no, no. I shall crush you!" she replied, figuring that's where he was, that's what he needed — tough talk for surviving recess in the real world with sturdier boys to whom Building Community was not quite the topic it was inside his progressive school or at home. Last time he'd come to visit they'd sorted her son Nick's toy soldiers into Keep, Give Away, and Dump. She'd offered the grand boy the Give Aways: a caveman hoisting a rock, a Greek wielding a spear, a Union soldier with attached cannon, a World War II group firing mortars: the whole dark history of the species set before them on a porch redolent with lilacs. He'd declined, confessing with lowered lids, "My mom doesn't let me have soldiers."

He rolled and bought St. James Place from the lower-middle-class purples. "Your turn," he said, bright-eyed for her demise.

She rolled and got to Electric Company, the single worst property on the board, worth nothing without its partner, Water Works. Never mind, in the real world, oil and water would soon be worth everything.

Handing over her first deed, the grand boy crowed: "I've got more property than you!"

"I will cream you," she replied.

He rolled doubles and bought Indiana in the middle-class reds and then one of the ominous yellows, Marvin Gardens. They had been her brother's favorite. Many times she'd met a sickening bankruptcy upon them.

"You're dead," he said.

"You are so, so mistaken, hombre," she replied. "It is you, you who are dead." A grandmother, even an artificial grandmother, can give you what you want and not have to live with the consequences.

She landed on Community Chest and paid a school tax of one hundred and fifty dollars. "I vill get you," she said, falling back on the German accent rife in the war films of her childhood.

He landed on the wealthiest side of the board and bought *her* favorite, the beautifully green and glowing Pennsylvania.

She landed on Go To Jail.

He rolled, passed Go, collected his two hundred bucks, and bought boring old Baltic. "Do you feel really awful?" he asked, with that terrible smile.

"I feel great," she announced with languid command. "Because soon I vill overcome you."

"You're so dead," he said.

"Watch this." She rolled and got to New York and bought it, even though he already had an orange property himself. "Now," she said, "how's about I give you some serious money for that worthless New Jersey you're sitting on?"

"How much?"

"Well, let's see. It cost you one-eighty. I'll give you three hundred."

"Are you kidding? You could get a set!"

"Eggzactly, pardner."

"Dream on."

He rolled and bought Illinois. Now he had two of the reds. She willed the dice to take her to the third red, and so put a crimp in his getting that set. But no, her roll took her straight past the reds into the yellows, Marvin Gardens to be exact. She paid him twenty-four dollars in rent money.

"A mere nothing," he shrugged. "Wait till it gets hotels."

"You'll need Ventnor first," she reminded him, a bit sharply. "And Atlantic."

"No problem. I creamed my father."

So it went. He acquired the red set and the green. She got a couple of railroads, Water Works, some singles, and two of the purples. Cheap stuff or not, the purples were her only chance for a set.

Next roll and he landed on the last purple. She was lost. But this time he'd spent almost all his money and she made him another offer: "I'll give you five hundred buckaroos to buy that lousy piece of purple on an alley covered with cat poop and non-biodegradable plastic bags."

"Are you kidding? That would give you a set!"

"Hey, you've already got *two* sets!" She hoped she wasn't whining. She did manage not to give a speech on justice and mercy.

Nothing doing — he mortgaged some property and bought the last purple. All sets were closed to her now. There was no hope at all. She was an African country in debt to the World Bank. She was a farmer in the Great Depression.

He called out, "Next time I go around Go, I'm putting houses on everything!"

Praying for socialism, she remembered her consciousness-raising group in the early years of feminism's second wave, when Minny Bauman had argued that they shouldn't let their kids play this capitalistic game at all and the group had split up over it.

He passed Go and bought a house for Indiana. "That'll be ninety dollars, if you land on it!" He was looking a little flushed.

"I ain't got no intention of landing on that."

"You gotta land on it sometime."

"I will cream you," she replied, though the tone was off and the accent gone.

On and on. Roll, play, pay him something. Roll, play, pay him something. Finally, as a model for good sportsmanship, she reached a place where she felt she could say — and did so with some relief — "I'm throwing in the towel, kiddo. I'm giving up, I'm knuckling under. Uncle! I'm crying uncle. It's over. You win. I lose. Good game. I'm dead." Alas, the relief of surrender was not to be hers.

He gave her a look of disbelief. "You've got to play to the end!" he explained, as if education could fix the world. "You've got to mortgage everything!"

She played to the end. She mortgaged everything. Her last dollar wasn't enough to cover her deficit. She was truly dead.

"I creamed you!"

She narrowed her eyes and managed to regain the right tone: "Next time, buddy, it is I who chr-eams you!"

He began to sort the money then paused. "Wanna play again right now?"

"Oh, no, no! Some other day. How about a little iced tea?"

"Okay." He gathered up the property, the tokens, his houses, his hotels. This was an improvement on her brother, who, bloated with cash, would kick the set away and scream, "Losers pick up!" She cheered herself on: *See? This boy is putting everything away, and neatly. There's progress in the world.* When he looked up, he said, "Shall I play my violin now?"

"Oh, lovely, I'll be right back."

She brought iced chamomile from the kitchen and a little plate of the ginger cookies her own grandmother, their shared ancestress, used to store in an earthenware jar in a dark pantry at a time when the hot war was over and the cold beginning, with its nuclear weapons waiting in the sky like unborn souls.

"They're good," he said. He drank half his tea and put the glass down. He picked up the violin case and opened it.

Taking a seat on a straight-backed chair, he fixed the chin rest to his half-size violin. He brought out the bow and settled himself into the posture he'd been taught. Raising the bow and with his eyes focused somewhere inside himself, inside his fingers, inside the hand that moved the bow, inside the head where his memory of the notes was stored, he played "Row, Row, Row Your Boat." He went on, playing "Frere Jacques," "Follow, Follow, Follow Me," and "Greensleeves." Just the one note of melody on the horsetail hairs of a bow pulled taut across strings made from the guts of some animal she couldn't remember. Deer? Pig? Or maybe they were synthetic now? There were occasional squeakings and failed notes and a kind of haze over the music. It took her awhile to figure out that he'd switched to "Jingle Bells."

"I haven't practiced for months," he explained. "My dad just got my violin fixed."

"It's good. I love it. Keep on."

"This is my favorite," he announced with his face tilted down to the instrument. "It's the famous Baytoenigh."

Baytoenigh? What was that? Had she heard right?

Stroking the bow again, he furthered his concentration in this room with its Swedish rug and light-filtering curtains before bringing from his shortened strings the exuberant notes of what she recognized as the "Ode to Joy" from Beethoven's Ninth. Ah, Baytoenigh, Of course. She watched the grand boy's thoughtful, vulnerable face; she listened to the triumphant hymn extolling a brotherhood of nations; yet what she saw in her mind's eye was a panorama of tall buildings collapsing like so many hotels on a board kicked askew and all this in the light of the recent rockets' red glare over Baghdad.

The nine-year-old face remained earnest and introspective as he played through the circling bars. A hymn of peace, was it enough for redemption? This arm held at the perfect angle, this chin set firmly on the chin rest? She thought of all the things this delicate crazy rational greedy loving species had created from the time of the ice to the time of global warming while other species were going extinct and yet somehow this one tree sloth or whatever, this chimpanzee, was growing up to be six billion people who didn't just drown in their own waste or shoot each other into small rotting pieces. They also played the violin.

Pru Pulls the Cord

After Cori's visit, Pru began to extend herself a bit. She signed up for Farmingdale's tag sale committee. She took herself to the pond for the afternoon Wine&Cheese held en plein air. One day she went over to the bin room at the Inn to haul out her patio furniture and there she met a woman with wonderfully thick white hair held back by combs. That's how Pru had intended to wear her hair when she got this old but it had thinned too much to hold any combs. The two became friends and Pru reported to Nikki with pride that her new friend Susan had taught philosophy at Wellesley.

Susan invited Pru to watch a DVD and soon they were watching together every other night. It was after they saw *Awakenings* that the two of them sat in Susan's book-lined living room drinking the first Jack Daniels over ice that Pru had consumed in decades.

"I figure nothing's wrong with dying," Susan said. "You just don't want to go first."

"Or last," Pru said, remembering her mother at ninety-eight.

"The middle's good. That's what I want. I see us as a bunch of coeval lemmings running toward a cliff. It wouldn't seem so scary in the middle of the bunch." Susan gave a little laugh. "Kind of like shoes."

"Shoes?" The icy liquor warmed Pru's throat.

"You know. It's best to be a size eight — right in the middle. Almost everybody's a size eight or eight and a half. It's a comfort."

"I wouldn't know. I'm a ten."

"Exactly my point. Safety in numbers. Be average, I say. Join hands and jump. Just like those sisters at the Twin Towers on 9/11."

"But they . . . ."

"I figure mid-eighties. That's the best time. Don't you think?"

It's after supper in late June, twilight, the children's hour, except there are no children on Farmingdale's carefully tended lawns, no sounds of their play, of their searching out what's hidden, of their calling for each other as dusk deepens into evening. Pru stands in her kitchen, placing warm brownies in a flowered tin. With tin in hand, she walks out her front door and makes her way over to Susan's front door. She picks up the brass knocker and brings it down softly, three times.

No sound of footsteps.

She tries again, with more force, because Susan *is* a little hard of hearing. She's got to be in there, though. *See you at seven* — Pru remembers saying that. Remembers it very clearly. Maybe Susan's having trouble loading the new Netflick? It's *Giant* with Elizabeth Taylor, a woman who put on weight at pretty much the same time and in the same places as Pru.

Still no footsteps.

Maybe Susan forgot? Pru tries the door. The latch loosens to the pressure of her thumb and allows her entry into a tiny foyer identical to her own. "Susan?" She leans in, calls out her friend's name. She steps inside. Silence meets her, and more than halfway.

She shuts the door behind her. "Hi there, Susan?" She continues calling as she walks past the living room and into the kitchen, with its avocado-tinted appliances just like her own. Susan's not here. Goosebumps appear on the back of Pru's neck. Something is reverberating, some current of distress, a reverberation below the threshold of her hearing. She sets the brownies on the counter, reenters the hall, gazes at the stairway that leads to the second floor.

Should she?

The stairs are carpeted and Pru walks silently up, knowing that the bedroom will be straight ahead. At least that's where it is in her condo. And yes, there it is, straight ahead. She enters the bedroom aglow with the evening's last light, the shades open to a view of the pond with its artificial-looking white birches.

Okay, she says to herself. Okay. The bathroom.

A few more steps and she stops, seeing the foot, a bare foot, and then there is Susan facedown on the floor, her head jammed against the base of the sink, her neck at a funny angle, the pale, pale skin. There's water in the tub, flat, unmoving. The bath mat is askew with what must have been a fall too quick for Susan's comprehension. Wasn't it? Oh please! Say it's so. She stands there.

Do.

Something.

Come on, she says to herself. You're no rookie when it comes to crisis. How many times did you get Cyrus up off the floor? That's not the job to be done here, though. She knows what she's looking at. Come on! She steps over Susan, resisting the temptation to stop and cover the naked body, to warm it with a bath towel. Too late for that. Careful not to slip in the skim of what must be urine on the linoleum, she stretches for the red cord that hangs near the toilet and pulls on it. Slowly, carefully, she backs out of the bathroom and into the bedroom, where the phone is already ringing. She picks it up to say, "Trouble, trouble here. In 152." A male voice asks a question to which she replies, "I'm afraid so." Then her legs give way and she drops to a seat on the bed. She's there when two brawny men arrive with the same kind of stretcher on folding metal legs that they brought up to the townhouses when Cyrus died. After the men take Susan away, Pru opens the drain in the bathtub and lets the water run out over her hand.

Cold.

It was so fast you didn't know. Right, Susan? Pru doesn't believe you can talk to the dead but she *feels* it to be possible and even if it's not, she likes the story of it, the story of immortality, the story of heaven. It's all so reassuring, like a giant children's storybook in bold acrylic colors.

Back in her own kitchen and having poured herself a glass of wine, Pru reaches for the wall phone. It's Tuesday night, Cori's yoga night, and Pru needs to talk to someone right away. Now. Now — as she faces her empty condo, the walk she must take up her own carpeted stairs, into her own bedroom. Just as she's about to key in her son's number, the phone rings. It's her granddaughter in Atlanta with a question: Is ten old enough to ride a horse?

"You've called the right grandmother," Pru says, pleased to have been the first consult, to have beaten out Grandma Bea, the overly strict. "Yes, indeed, I do believe that a girl of ten should be able to ride a horse . . . . He doesn't? You can remind that father of yours that he was pretty good at the rudder of a sailboat when *he* was ten. Now, sweetie, could you . . . ?"

"I already tried that," the girl replies. "He says you were holding the rudder."

"You tell him I've got a picture to prove it." On any other day, this would be a treat to prolong. Not tonight. "I'm sorry, sweetie, I need to talk to your Dad."

But another child's voice comes on, a younger and mournful one. "He's so sick. He won't eat. Not even the catnip crackers."

"Well," Pru says, relieved the sick one is not her son. "Have you tried magic thoughts?"

"What's that?"

"You close your eyes and see just what you want to see." A little dizzy now, Pru lowers herself onto a stool with a seat too small in circumference to fully receive her buttocks. "Say, for instance, you shut your eyes and see Tinker running around. Eating his food. Playing with his jingle ball . . . ."

"What's the magic part?"

"Oh, you're too smart for me, sweetie! Try it and see! And now, can I *please* have a word with your Dad?" She waits for the sound of shared memory, of long connection. She waits to be taken care of, to be the comforted and not the comforter.

"Charlie? This awful thing happened, and I wanted to hear your voice."

"What's that, Mum?"

They speak for a few minutes but Charlie and Stephie are on their way to a club meeting. After she hangs up, Pru remembers that she left the brownies at Susan's. She's not going over there. Not now. She'll get them in the morning. She hangs up and climbs upstairs. She gets into bed with her clothes on. Doesn't lie down. Sits up with the light on. Here is her rose-tinted wall just like Susan's, her window onto the pond just like Susan's, her bathroom with its door ajar just like Susan's. Her tub. Her floor. She shudders. Then, propped up against her pillows, she congratulates Susan. Nice job, Susan! Eighty-three, just what you wanted. She herself is only seventy-four. She snaps off her bedside lamp.

An hour later she gets up and takes a sleeping pill.

Where's Nikki?

The plumbing system at the Elder Horizons Camp in southern Spain where Nikki was teaching *Data Collection for Family History* broke down two days before the end of the session. Most of the pensioners and teachers cut out for the bus to Madrid but Nikki had a Saturday flight booked at the tiny airport nearby, as did one young Douglas from London who was teaching *Introduction to the Digital Camera*. Over a last desolate dinner, the camp director suggested these two spend the next day and night in Granada and get back Friday night in time to pack for their Saturday morning flights. "I'd like tha'," Douglas said in his vowel-focused English. "Me too," Nikki said. So the next morning this unlikely pair set out together with their backpacks.

They managed to board a bus and pay for tickets with the few Spanish words Nikki possessed and each found a window seat among the many that were available. A good beginning, she thought: He won't intrude on me and I won't intrude on him. He's a young man, needs his freedom. It was a relief not to be talking, not to be laboring to keep her English simple or to understand the Spanish that had drifted about the classroom as women spoke to each other of their lives.

She turned her attention to the string of pastel-tinted seaside vacation condominiums outside her window. They ran without interruption through towns where Phoenicians and Jews and Greeks and Romans and Arabs had lived. One town offered a wealth of silver, the next featured sheep's wool, and every town grew oranges, olives, and almonds. She didn't understand how this dry soil could grow anything at all. It didn't look capable of supporting much but tourists' bocce courts and an occasional shopping center.

Then the bus turned westward, away from the sea, and slowly began to rise through Vera, where the Romans finally beat the Carthaginians, on up to the larger town of Cuevos, with its bright clean supermarket and its Colors of Benetton. Across the aisle Douglas sat with his eyes closed, listening on headphones to something that managed to make it through the dark, thick dreadlocks to his ears.

Some people don't care about history, Nikki told herself. No past, no future, just a thick present that stretches out to either side. Sometimes she wished she could be like them.

Instead, here she was, checking her watch to see if they were on time for Cuevos. What did it matter?

Across the aisle Douglas appeared content.

After Cuevos, the road continued to ascend into the mountains and soon they were passing through a wide and gently sloping valley between two mountain ridges. Snow appeared on the southern ridge, the ridge outside Douglas's window.

"Douglas," she called softly across the aisle, "it's the Sierra Nevada." He stirred himself. "Wha'?"

She gestured to the view. "Sierra Nevada."

He got out his tiny silver camera but didn't shoot anything.

The towns became smaller and farther apart. Crops lay hidden under white plastic. With the dusty dark green of roadside shrubs and hills rising, it looked like California, southern California. An orange grove appeared, with the bright globes standing out against dark leaves. Whole hillsides of white flowering almond trees in neat rows. Remnants of what could be a Roman aqueduct.

Another big town, she couldn't find its name in the signage: *Ayuntamiento, meubles, immobiliari?* Those didn't sound like the names of towns. *Almanzora?* Perhaps. There was stone here — the quarrying, transporting, selling, and working of stone. There was wood, too. Stores displayed wooden furniture in their windows. Stone, wood, these are industries a human being can understand. Unlike the digital camera.

Douglas pulled the curtain over his window, cutting out the sun and the view.

In Parchena the oranges were falling off the trees and lying like prizes on the earth below. After this, there was no stop for miles and miles of planted fields, of terraces. This was Andalusia, which she knew to have been the breadbasket of the Phoenicians and of the Romans and of all conquerors or traders since. It had been settled even earlier by people who survived the Ice Age in the caves of these hills and who, when the ice melted, came out to hunt and fish and ever so slowly to upgrade hunting into herding and gathering into planting. Oh, she did love to know these things about time passing.

When they pulled into the sheltered bus stop in the big city of Baza, Douglas stood up. "D'ya know the word for bathroom?" he asked her.

"*Baños*," she replied and off he went.

Her younger son had worn dreadlocks like Douglas's. Now he ran a basil farm in Vermont, his fields crossed and bypassed by green plastic watering hoses, the greenhouse itself humid and sweet smelling. Health stores from Hartford to Boston bought his produce and lately he was taking Internet orders. He'd sported blondish dreads when he went off at twenty-four on his youthful who-shall-I-be travels, returning at twenty-six with short, curly hair and a sun-browned, muscular body. They'd missed his entire twenty-fifth year.

Douglas reappeared in the aisle and regained his seat as the bus pulled out of Parchena. Nikki checked her watch;

time for lunch. She opened her plastic wrap: hard-boiled egg, apple, bread, and the last of the marmalade from the staff refrigerator. Douglas was peeling his egg. Then he stopped. Holding it in one hand, he photographed it with the other.

Eventually the bus moved downhill in its approach to Guadix, and the snowy mountains began to loom higher and closer. A Christian church appeared. Christianity had been established here long before the Muslims came to plant Islam, which the Catholic Kings to the north eventually overthrew. Now the secular came into view: shops, a Renault dealership, a Delta Air Lines office. Next, fields on all the high slopes and once in a while the black hole of a cave opening in the side of a hill. Some of the caves had doors, one with a white wooden frame around it, painted with flowers. In another hour they began to descend again and there ahead of them lay Granada. She checked her watch. Right on time. She got out her sheet of instructions — *number 33 bus to Plaza Nueva, walk to the hostel on Cuesta Gomerez.*

Douglas hadn't opened his eyes. When almost everyone else had gotten off, he stood and shouldered his pack. "Where to?" he asked her, this young man on his travels. She said, "I thought we'd try the information booth."

They managed to get on the right bus and move down the aisle past four blond girls from somewhere north, each with a huge suitcase at her feet and a cat on her lap. No, of course not, not cats — only folded, fur-lined jackets. The girls were staring at Douglas.

She was suddenly aware that she was moving among white people with a young man of mixed blood at her side. At Horizons they'd been bound together as the only staffers whose mother tongue was English. Race and age may separate but language binds. She felt protective of him. He was a handsome young man with a strong sense of himself, and with an appealing gentleness as well. Still, she had no idea how he might feel on being surrounded by whites staring at him. Then she realized it was not his skin but his elaborate dreads that were fetching the gazes and that he'd probably designed his hair for this very effect. Matt had admitted as much when he'd sported dreads.

She saw from her map that the cathedral would be on the right and she held out the map to show Douglas exactly where. He paid it no mind, bending down to look out the window at actual rather than symbolic buildings. Suddenly he announced, "There 'tis." She headed toward the front but he touched her on the arm and pointed to the back door that was mandatory for exits and they made it out a second before the door wheezed shut. We travel well together, she thought.

Then they were in Granada, standing on a corner with people hurrying by, taking in the smell of car exhaust and the constant farting of motorcycles.

"What now?" he said.

"Well, I'm going to check into the hostel the director recommended." She'd heard Douglas tell the director that he wasn't sure where he'd stay in Granada, maybe he'd just wander about. She'd taken that to mean he wanted to be on his own. And so did she; that was the key to total immersion travel. So she said, "And you'll be off to photograph in the Albaycín, won't you?" He'd mentioned an interest in the white houses and narrow streets of the Moorish section of the city.

"Dunno. Maybe I'll come with you."

"Okay," she said, surprised. For all his cool he might be a bit unsure of himself in a foreign city. They started walking toward a statue in the square. "It's Ferdinand and Isabella!" she exclaimed. Well, it wasn't. It was Isabella and Christopher Columbus. Columbus was kneeling to present something — America? — to the seated queen. Oh, so much history right here. She hadn't known that Isabella or Columbus had anything to do with Granada. Douglas was finally studying the map she'd given him. No, he was handing it back to her and pointing to a sign so far off she couldn't read it.

"There 'tis," he said. "I see it with my eagle eye." She laughed and followed him to the hostel. The woman at the desk had no English and so she drew Douglas diagrams of two rooms, one with private bath and one with shared bath. While he studied the diagrams, the clerk turned to Nikki: Did they want a room for one or for two people? Embarrassed, she raised a single finger. But what a lover this boy would make for someone fifty years younger in body, as well as in what was once called soul. Happily, Douglas hadn't understood the clerk's question and soon they were upstairs and standing on the marble floor between their facing rooms.

"I'm going up to the Alhambra in a couple of minutes," she said. "What's your plan?"

"I'll go, too," he said, surprising her again.

"Okay. Five minutes then?"

Her room was tiled in green, with an elegant bathroom and shuttered doors that opened onto a small balcony over the Plaza Nueva. Taking the heavier items out of her backpack, she tied a nylon parka around her waist and they were off to the tourist bus that would take them up the steep hill to the sultan's palace. At the top they bought ten-euro tickets.

"Bit pricey," he said.

"Hey, we did it, no snags."

"Guess so." He still sounded a little lost.

"Well, I'll be back at the hostel about eight," she told him. "I'll knock on your door. If you feel like going out to dinner, we can. If not, I'll go alone."

"Awright then. Here's where we split." He waved and started off.

Following her map, she soon reached the sultan's palace, where she bought an audio tour. Holding it to her ear, she entered the great reception hall, where petitioners from distant places had waited to see the sultan or his staff at this, the seat of Muslim power in the medieval West. Next, to the room of the scribes and, finally, into the room that held the sultan's judgment seat. Here sat the top man of Andalusian Islam, pronouncing fates. Off with the hand, the tongue, the head! Now that she'd heard on TV an actual tape of a screaming man getting his head sawn off, the prospect transfixed her. Of course there would be violence where there was such tempting agricultural and mineral wealth. Ferdinand and Isabella had taken Andalusia from the Muslims by the sword, and now Al Qaeda dreamed of regaining it with car bombs and of renewing a Caliphate spread round the world.

Outside she reached the Alcázar, the oldest building in the complex, an army barracks, the home of Muslim, and then Christian, force. She climbed to the top of the watchtower, where flags were waving and where the great bell of Christian triumph hung. She looked out over the vastness of the Sierra Nevada and the fertile plains below. Young travelers teemed about her and she hoped Douglas had found some friends among such as these.

Back down on the Plaza Nueva, she discovered an Internet station larger than any she'd ever seen — maybe a hundred fifty people at the monitors. She took a seat between a well-coifed, executive-looking woman in western dress and a man in a robe and a turban. Cyberspace rewarded her with a cryptic note from her older son. *Good news here, Mom. Will save for your return.* She shot back *Nick! What a teaser! I'm in Granada and the guy next to me is filling his screen with Arabic. I'm trying not to think he's the local Al Qaeda cell.* Pru sent a reminder about the August book club meeting and Nikki replied *I'm here in Granada with a young man and I'm falling in love, halfway between mother and grandmotherly love.*

. . .

She got back to the hostel just before eight and knocked on Douglas's door. He'll be gone, she thought. Off with newfound friends. But the door opened. He'd had a good day, couldn't quite say where he'd been in the Moorish section's twisting, hilly streets. He'd seen some young African men selling objects off sheets placed on the street but every now and then they'd answer a cell phone and quickly make everything disappear into pockets and backpacks. It was a good place, Albaycín. He was hungry.

They walked the strip of tourist bars on the plaza and stood in front of a restaurant, studying the posted menu. It took some time for them to discover that the daily special was not four different things to eat but the same thing in French, Spanish, English, and German. It was pork, any way you looked at it. They both chose the chickpea soup to start. He chose the potatoes; she, the salad. While they waited for their food, he asked her if she wanted to see some of his photographs and when she said yes, he handed her the tiny silver camera and told her where to press the button.

There was a terrific shot of his hard-boiled egg, half peeled. And a startling one of the lock on the back of a bathroom door. "It was so chunky," he explained. "I had to shoot it." There were shots of the African men standing in slouches against the wall, wearing their red embroidered Jackie O. hats. A whole series of them in different postures, gathering up their goods, secreting them. There was a dog sitting in the sun beside his master — an old man who was sketching the traditional view across the Rio Dorra to the palaces and the watchtower. Douglas had a good eye for composition and color.

"You're a good photographer," she said.

"Bit discouraged," he allowed. He confessed he wasn't getting anywhere in the freelance life and had to support himself as a computer techie.

"Keep working."

"Don't give up, you mean?"

"Don't give up."

This was another woman's son, a woman who was probably missing Douglas as much as she'd missed Matt during the year of his travels. Tonight it was as if she'd somehow managed to meet up with her own son as he made his way years ago from Naples to Prague and down to Gaza. She finished off her glass of rioja. According to the menu, there'd be fruit for dessert, and when the waiter slapped down an orange and a dull steel knife in front of each of them, they both laughed.

"This is why it's so cheap," Douglas said. "We're the labor."

When the orange peels lay curled on their plates and the Spanish night beckoned, Nikki said, "We're near an Internet station. If you want to check your e-mail."

"What'll you be doin', then?"

"I'll be going back to the hotel. Got to read the guidebook and see what I missed today."

"Awright. I'll take a peek at the Internet place."

Was he taking care of *her?*

She made her way back to the hostel and up to the pleasant

room, where she got into her silk pajamas and plumped up the pillows in one of the beds. She didn't fall immediately to sleep. She lay there until she heard footsteps stopping at the room across the hall. He was back, safe. She could sleep.

In the morning Douglas knocked on her door and they agreed to meet at four outside the Internet station. From there they'd head back to the Elder Horizons Camp.

"Don't be late," she said.

He struck out toward the Albaycín for more photographs. She had her day in view: tea and a biscuit, a look at the sepulchers of Ferdinand and Isabella, a swing around the Arab shops, a bite of lunch, then up to the Museum of Archeology.

The sepulchers were splendidly ornate, Isabella with her heavenward gaze and Ferdinand with his sword. Beside them lay their mad daughter Joanna with her husband Philip. It was said that Joanna had opened her husband's casket each night for years to kiss the dear departed goodnight. Her poor parents lay watchful beside her, still looking out for her, even in death. You own a big chunk of the known world and discover the New World, but you cannot make a mad daughter well.

Pulling off her sunglasses she stepped down the *Entrada* stairs to the crypt where the actual bones of these royals rested in simple coffins. A young man stood at the railing looking in at them. Death seems so impossible to the young. To the old it's as common as spent teabags. Isabella may even have longed for it. In heaven Joanna might be okay. She turned and walked up the *Salida* stairs and practically into a tortuous scene of the Crucifixion. The coldness of stone buildings and the realities of extreme religious belief were getting to her.

She needed food, nothing Spanish today, maybe pizza or pasta. She needed a bathroom. On the Plaza Nueva she began to peer at the menus pictured on boards set here and about. The inevitable waiter appeared: "Señora, menu, full menu, seven-fifty euro, see picture here. Pasta tuna, pasta Bolognese, and this one, carbonara."

"Yes, yes," she said. Carbonara, that had been her husband's favorite. She hadn't eaten it for years on account of its cream content. She pointed to the picture of a plate of pasta Bolognese and asked if he had a bathroom.

"Yes, yes, lady, sit down."

Well, of course. He needed to be sure she'd pay. She could wait. So she sat and he brought the menu and showed more pictures of food. The Bolognese had meat in it. Veal. As soon as he'd gone into the kitchen she began to worry about mad cow disease. But the warmth of the sun was a blessing. A raggedly dressed man was playing a panpipe as he walked among the tables. A cheerful Chinese-looking girl was ordering various plates for her friends.

A glass of red, a basket of bread, and a plate of pasta with tomato sauce and cheese arrived. The pasta was better than she'd expected and she was relieved to find no meat in it. She ate slowly, looking across the plaza and up the steep hill to the Alcázar and its watchtower. Three flags were flying on it.

From down here the medieval barracks looked like the very fist of oppression. She tried to imagine all the people who'd lived here on the streets below it, both the Jews and the Moors who'd looked up at the fortress the day they learned they were to be expelled by the Catholic Kings, their property taken, the doors of their own homes shut to them. What it would be like to look up there and see the flag of radical Islam flying? More ruined children, bombed houses, streets full of corpses? For a while perhaps, but new generations would arise who might be able to shrug their shoulders and go on living, pretty much as the Spanish and the tourists were living now.

She found the restroom and, when she came out, gave her check and some money to the cook who was standing at the range behind the counter.

"How was food?" he asked.

"It was good, very good!"

"You are lovely u-wooman."

She laughed and wondered if he'd somehow stolen her passport while distracting her with a compliment. But when she walked into the sunlight and toward the archeological museum, she found herself smiling at another possibility. Maybe he was only making up for the lack of veal in her meal?

At the museum she examined carefully knapped stones, pottery jars and bowls — things she usually loved to linger over. But here in the stone mansion, she began to feel cold and hurried past the Phoenicians' gift of an alphabet she knew and the curving calligraphy of an alphabet she didn't know.

Somewhere in these rooms she paused before a life-sized stone carving of a seated woman, dug up from ancient Baza: plump, wealthy, dressed in a decorated gown, wearing earrings in the shape of boxes. You can see her today in Beverly Hills or on the Champs. She's what you get when you control the food supply, the water, the oil.

It was three-thirty and her mind was not at all on the past.

She had to meet Douglas. She left the museum, stopped at the hostel for her backpack, moved out into the sun again. It was still early but she thought it worth checking inside the Internet place. He might be in there reading e-mail. She entered the shop and looked around but there was no young man with dreads. He wasn't here. And why should he be? It was only quarter of four. She left and walked around a couple of blocks, then back to the Internet station. Once again, he wasn't there.

What would she do if he didn't appear? Was he okay? She mustn't worry. But what if he'd gotten caught in some racial thing involving the African men with their forbidden street sales? What if he were in jail? How would she find him? Don't be ridiculous. He isn't even late! It's only five of four. She spent three more minutes looking at inlaid tile boxes displayed by a street vendor and then abruptly headed back to the Internet place. He won't be there, she told herself, readying for the worst. But when she rounded the last corner, there he was, sitting on a bench near the shop, a young man on his travels, waiting for her.

What's Wrong with Chessa?

"Relax, kid," Chessa said to the dog standing unsteadily on the passenger seat beside her. "You *love* Bed and Bowl, remember?" Apparently he did, because when they got to the farmhouse with the great fence around it, he jumped happily from the car and ran to Fletcher, a dog lady wearing a red bandana. Standing in the snow, they discussed their arrangements and Chessa wrote a check, handed it over, climbed back into the car, and headed north to Vermont. Traffic was light, as expected on a weekday after the holidays, and at just about suppertime she arrived to her single room at the White Bounty Ski Lodge.

In the family-style dining room she snagged an empty seat at a trestle table full of too many kids for the single man and woman who appeared to be their parents. Some kind of blended family. Eight children, she counted: half blond, half dark-haired, like a litter of puppies born to a bitch who'd mated twice the same day.

"How's the hot dog?" she asked the girl of nine or ten sitting to her left.

"I should have had quiche," the girl replied, turning her face away.

Chessa surveyed the view beyond the table. She was the oldest person in the room.

Next day she slid one foot and then the other into hard plastic boots, remembering the classic black leather lace-up Henkes from Switzerland she'd begged her parents to give her that last Christmas at college. They'd complied, but she'd never worn them. Mostly, she'd smoked and slept that semester, after the loss of her first true love. Well, she was over men, at last!

With her feet stuck in their rigid yellow prisons, she hoisted her skis to her shoulder and made her way to the lift. At the top of the mountain, she chose a fairly easy trail and stood surveying the world before heading down. She took in the enormous horizon line, the hills, the great Out There, all blue-white under a blue-white sky, the vastness that, if you kept your eyes up, was empty of everything but sky, snow, mountain.

She shook out her legs, the left, the right, her feet immobile in the yellow boots. Frigid air found its way between her jacket and her scarf, hitting her neck. With ski poles looped over her wrists, she struggled to retie her scarf. It had been a year since she'd skied downhill, and a small doubt began sniffing around her. Yes, around *her*, Francesca Waterford, captain of her ski team, the woman who did not hesitate. Go! she told herself.

And down she went, wobbly on a sticky bit of slush, late for the first turn, catching up for the second, and then it all came back to her and she was flooded with the ease and pleasure of it. Down she glided, turn by turn; here she was, as young, as strong, as foolhardy as ever.

On her fifth run down and almost at the bottom where the trail flattened out, something happened to her left leg. It went briefly dead. Not as if it were asleep, not as if it suffered a cramp. No, this was some other sensation, one she'd never experienced. Still, she managed to ski straight ahead — her right leg bearing her weight and her left ski sliding along on top of the snow. And then the sensation vanished and she stood at the bottom aware of both legs firmly beneath her.

It must be the damn boots, the way they pinched her ankles. She unclamped her skis and headed for the hot tub.

At supper, she chose a small table in a corner of the room far from the crowded tables by the windows with their view of scores of skiers descending the mountain under fluorescent lights. A twenty-year-old approached, bearded and with brown eyes like her second husband's.

"Excuse me," he said. "Is this chair free?"

"Oh, yes." She smiled. "Please, sit." But he only nodded

and picked up the chair and whisked it to the other side of the room.

It happened again the next day in the middle of the afternoon, that strange sensation in her left leg. This time she was riding in the gondola up the mountain and stayed inside to ride back down. Best to quit early anyway. She wanted to be full of energy when Emily showed up from Burlington.

Uncharacteristically, Chessa asked Emily to drive them to the restaurant where she'd made a reservation. No trestle tables at this place, no large families, just Emily, as tall as her mother. And with good news, good news for Chessa, that is, sad for Emily: The software man was being transferred to Saint Louis.

"I stayed with him too long," Emily said, a striped scarf softening a black, gold-buttoned jacket.

"You've got time. Plenty of time." In reality there wasn't so much, but never mind. "You'll find someone."

On Thursday Chessa chose a lower and more open hill, in case her leg should go funny again. But everything was fine. Even supper was good and, after the twice-baked potatoes and the two tiny lamb chops, she was invited to join the crowd at one of the trestle tables, a crowd of middle-aged social workers from some agency down in Brooklyn, up here to celebrate someone's fiftieth birthday.

Fifty? Pah!

She engaged in small talk with the woman next to her,

a woman with spiked red hair. On the verge of spilling out her news about Emily to a stranger or giving a description of her problem with her leg, she was stopped by the red-haired woman's announcement: "Any minute now Dexter is going to get us into this thing called charades. You ever hear of it?"

"I was a champ," Chessa replied, warmed by images of Thanksgivings and Christmases with aunts and uncles folding up slips of paper and acting out words or phrases without the use of spoken language. A kind of sophistication had exuded from those long-gone adults, as she and her young cousins found themselves initiated into the games of the grown-up world. Now here at Bounty, she was being invited into those same secrets again — only this time it was entry back into the prime years being offered, not into the future, only into the past.

When she managed to act out the movie title *Necromancer*, everyone cheered. She'd never heard of the film and evoked it by pointing to her neck and then miming a dancer, a ball gown, and a kiss. Nor could she guess the words other players were trying to express. She didn't get their references. She didn't know Mr. Spock, only Dr. Spock, whose manual on child-rearing she'd been reading while in the maternity ward after producing Emily. She'd read all the way to adolescent rebellion before they put the twenty-inch newborn into her arms.

Friday she skied till noon, packed up her little red Kia, and took off for home, feeling pleased about Emily, refreshed by what skiing she'd managed, and full of a heartiness that lasted till she pulled past the mobile homes into her own driveway and opened her passenger side door to extract the skis. Reaching into the car, she found her left arm going dead in that same funny way. The skin of her head prickled. She swallowed, took as big a breath as she could, and lifted the skis out of the car and into the garage. Then, eyes on the road, she drove one-handed straight to Bed and Bowl. The wiry black dog danced at her arrival and jumped into the passenger seat. Turning the car, she said, "Those boots were too stiff for my leg, that's all it is. Innit, Jack?" She didn't mention her arm.

Why Is Pru Still Lying on the Floor?

How fast it goes, more than a year now since the death of Susan and the shock has receded, leaving Pru with a pulsing whisper: *Get ready! Get ready!* It's an urgency reminiscent of her financial advisor's when he insisted she sell her town-house. She really must figure out what to do with her papers. Cyrus's love letters would be wrong for the children. All those study notes from when she gave piano lessons, boring. And she must review her estate plan — laws and passwords change all the time, leaving you locked out of your own memory. She opts for none of these chores. She subscribes to Netflix instead and invites her new neighbor Doris to a weekly film fest. But the whisper comes back strong when her doctor tells her she's got to lose twenty pounds or risk a stroke. She knows stroke. Cyrus. Wheelchair. Drooling.

So this time she does something.

It's hot when she heads out to the admin building to discover what Farmingdale offers by way of health and fitness programs. She is certainly not going to get into her car and drive to the YWCA at the other end of town. No, no, everything she needs is right here at Farmingdale. When she reaches an intersection in the cement paths, she sees a tall man approaching; it's the widower who bought her townhouse. Wes? Was that his name? Win?

"How's it going?" He stops, inquires. He's wearing a baseball cap against the sun.

She too has come to a standstill. "Can't complain. I'm off to the gym." His eyes are blue, like Cyrus's.

"Oh yes, my doctor's always at me about that."

"Whose isn't?" She tries for a joke, realizes she's tilting her head to one side, like a teenager, coy. After all, she has not had a private conversation with a man for — how long now?

He touches his cap, heads up the hill.

So his doctor wants him to exercise? What's he got? She turns to study his gait. He walks fine. She can imagine herself falling into step easily beside him. With Cyrus she'd be trying to keep up with his electric scooter. Or the scooter would be nipping at her heels. Oh, she wasn't good enough to Cyrus those last years! But he got so heavy, it took half an hour to lever him up off the floor when he fell. Plus enough pillows and footstools to shame the hydraulic engineers of the ancient Egyptians.

At the Admin Office, she looks over the brochures and picks up *Senior Fitness.* She scans it — not that she actually considers herself a senior. She has the extra poundage. She has the rosy cheeks of rosacea. She has the whitened and thinning hair. She's even got the start of a bald spot. Yet, what she yearns for is to be invited out to play.

August comes, a time in New England when foliage begins to look faintly like garbage. It's humid. The air hangs like laundry. The heat of the earth comes up through the soles of Pru's sandals and her loose gardening pants flap against bare shins. She doesn't hurry, even though she's late to her aerobics class. Best not to hurry anymore.

Music barrels out the gym door — *Dancin' in the Street! Dancin' in the Street!* — and the petite, ponytailed instructor in spandex is already calling out the marching orders. Inside, Pru slips off her sandals and laces up her exercise sneakers to the staccato beat that ricochets around the room where a dozen or so similarly shod women are marching on a gleaming hardwood floor. In the middle of the women stands a single man, Homer.

Everybody loves Homer. He's ninety-six. That's old enough to have fathered some of these women during a careless hayride on a summer night in the long ago, had he been that kind of boy. He has outlived a wife, two children, seven dogs and as many cars, switching from Fords to Toyotas midway through. He's the last of his generation to go over the cliff, Pru figures. A perfect size twelve, as Susan would have put it.

She slips into the empty space that's left beside Homer and begins to march, careful of her right hip. It's not arthritis. And if it is, she doesn't want to know. Hot in here, despite the air conditioning. She's lucky her gardening pants aren't elasticized at the bottom. She studies Homer's feet. He isn't really marching. He's just lifting one foot a bit and then the other. Well, actually, he's only lifting his heels.

"Step, touch!" Erica calls out. Raised a Methodist, this instructor considers her work at Farmingdale to be her foreign mission.

Pru steps high and pumps her arms to the beat and wail of *Sherry, Sherry Baby!* Homer lifts his whole foot now but doesn't step from side to side as everyone else is doing. Pru must take tiny steps so as not to crash into him.

"Hamstrings!"

Pru bends her right leg back toward her buttocks, then her left leg, moving to the beat. Directly in front of her, an admirably thick, if grey, braid bounces on bare, unfamiliar shoulders. Someone new? From the townhouses probably, or she'd know her.

The door in the front of the room opens. It's the blue-eyed man who bought her townhouse, the man she ran into several weeks ago. He's still sporting the baseball cap he was wearing then. Indoors? Is he going bald? She incorporates what might be taken for a wave into her arm movements. He evidences no recognition and settles on the other side of the room. *Pretty Woman* starts up and Pru remembers when she was one.

Erica comes to a standstill, orders a deep breath for all, and, as she inhales in demonstration, raises her arms over her head. They all inhale, raise their arms. A pause in the steady thrum of rock provides just enough silence for a strange wheezing to be heard. Is someone having trouble breathing? Is someone taking a last breath? They stand in place, arms high in the air, as if this were a game of freeze tag. Then Erica laughs and says, "It's just the dehumidifier!" Released to life, they drop their arms and break formation, noisily making their way to where they've stashed their water bottles.

Pru is about to go over and welcome the blue-eyed man to the class but that new woman, Greybraid, is pulling a red-and-white-striped towel back and forth across the nape of her neck like a triumphant athlete and making her way straight to him. It's Win, not Wes, Pru decides and stops her progress toward him abruptly when she hears Greybraid saying, "Hey there, can you spare a bit of water?" The man nods, the man smiles, the man hands over his bottle. He must have been a lady-killer. Maybe he still is — only now the ladies really do die.

And Then He Kissed Me pumps up and Erica calls for "Grapevine!"

Homer doesn't do grapevine. He could trip over his feet. He could fall to his death or simply break a hip. When they all clap their hands and turn ninety degrees, he just stands there. When they reverse direction, he takes a little step to the right, ending up where he started.

"Nice job, Homer!" Erica calls out.

Doo Wah Diddy Diddy offers its promise of total possessive love, and it's time for sashay. How Pru loves to sashay! It's so much like dancing. She stands as tall as she can so no one, including Win, could possibly see her tiny bald spot. Cyrus wouldn't have cared about her bald spot. He would have loved her anyway. Her girlish dreams had been of Heathcliff and Cathy, one hundred percent commitment, not even death doing them part. Though her innocence has given way before such things as political choices, annoying habits of speech, one suspected infidelity, and numerous infections from indwelling catheters, she finds that the sashay restores her to romance. She takes two steps lightly to the right with a substantial skip between. Then back the other way. Sashay gives her the illusion that she's back in college among friends who are so young they don't even imagine the day they'll have tiny magnets on their refrigerators holding up the crayonings of their grandchildren. They themselves are the grandchildren.

Erica calls for another water break and Pru can't help noticing that Greybraid is approaching Win a second time. She watches as the two stand half a foot apart, facing each other, their chests rising a bit. She watches as Win unscrews his water bottle and offers it to Greybraid, as Greybraid takes it and raises it to her lips, swallows, and hands it back, as Win takes a longer swallow and resettles the cap. It's all over. They have drunk from the same bottle. They have brushed away all thoughts of germ theory; they have thrown caution out their townhouse windows. Forget it.

I Only Wanna Be with You begins and Pru screws the cap back onto her own water bottle a bit aggressively. She's glad she's not still in college. This would have thrown her. But not now. She knows whose queen she is. Let them eat cake! She tightens the drawstring on her gardening pants and it dawns on her where she can buy a sympathy card for the death of her granddaughters' cat.

"Balance work!"

Hearts racing, they scurry to the railing that runs along the wall. Not Homer. Homer doesn't scurry. Homer gets there in his own sweet time. Only Greybraid can actually do what Erica is demonstrating — stand on one leg and raise the other straight out to hip height without holding on to anything. At the railing Pru actually gets her leg up almost level with her hip. Homer manages a couple of inches.

"Nice work, Homer!" Erica calls. Annoyed, Pru lowers her leg.

Soon they are standing beside the mats they've scattered on the floor, holding their two- and three-pound weights. Damp with sweat, Pru pushes her reluctant, weighted arms up and down, sideways and back, until at last it's time to kneel and unfold her unwieldy self along the sticky mat. A scone would be perfect right now, coffee. Someone farts. Pru hopes it's Greybraid.

She's getting a little winded and her hip can no longer be ignored. There won't be time for a nap after lunch. It's book club night and she hasn't finished reading the book, can't even remember its title. If she's lucky, they may not have much time for a real discussion anyway, there being so much else to talk about. Nikki's e-mail, to start. Pru remembers *that* perfectly. *Dear Bookies, I won't make the meeting on the 14th. I'll be in Seattle waiting for Nick and Traci to come back from China with my new granddaughter! Promised to stay till at least one of them is sleeping through the night.* Then Chessa with her chemotherapy . . . oh, *The World Without Us,* that's it! She's got the title. A good start. And, oh yes, without humans to run the pumps in the subways of Manhattan, the tunnels would fill in a week with the water of underground rivers. She remembers that. And without humans to clean out the soil and seed that birds drop between the metal plates of the George Washington Bridge, the bridge would fall into the Hudson in a mere two years. Sometimes Pru gets an unpleasant picture in her head of her own grandchildren, Pearl and Amanda, in corpse-strewn Atlanta, surviving in the resource wars, tattered and barefoot, fighting over a pail of water. When it's her turn to suggest a book, she means to ask that they reread *Wuthering Heights.* Oh, no, they don't read fiction anymore.

The Chapel of Love starts up, and Pru remembers how

Cyrus used to sing it in the shower, when he could still stand up. Erica speeds about the room, dimming the ceiling lights for a full minute of what she calls Meditation, although she calls it Corpse Position in her class downtown. She slips a new CD into the slot, and into the dimmed room come wafts of plinkity plink, as a soft-voiced Hawaiian plays the ukulele and sings *Somewhere over the Rainbow* until it morphs into *What a Wonderful World*. In Pru's eyes tears well up. That's what everybody sang at Cyrus's memorial. Ever in charge, he had designed his own service around a CD of Louie Armstrong singing this very song. Louie, Louis. Now it was always Louis, with the *s*. Not to her generation, to her generation it would always be Louie and here she was an old woman lying on a mat and where was Cyrus? They had danced to Louie, they had danced to the Duke, at the pier on Old Orchard Beach where they'd first met, waiting tables, and later at college when she took the train for football weekends, marshaling a suitcase full of party clothes. She in a shimmering cloud of blue net, Cyrus in a cummerbund — the Lindy, the two-step, even the Charleston of their parents' time. Generation after generation over the cliff, just as Susan said. Lying here on her well-padded backside, Pru takes in the song as if Cyrus were singing it to her from the other side, singing it in a soft and recently acquired Hawaiian accent such as they might actually speak in heaven. And why not? Oh, even though she doesn't believe in heaven, she can see it before her, sandy beaches, radiant sky, billowy clouds, and on one of them, standing, Cyrus, her only lover, perfectly restored and waiting for her. Really! What a wonderful world!

The lights snap on, the class rises to seated positions at the varying speeds their flexibilities allow. At Erica's direction, all but one of them raise their arms and take in a last deep breath, the breath that separates us from the dead. They put their palms together in the nation's newly ubiquitous gesture of respect before rising from the floor at their various speeds. Homer pats his face with a big white handkerchief. "Have a good day!" Erica calls, as the folks for Chair Yoga drift into the room past the outgoing class, which leaves in twos or threes, heading for coffee.

Only Pru doesn't get up, not just yet. She wants a minute more, flat on the floor, a minute more to get hold of the picture she's forming of all of them together, all the generations in sequence, walking hand in hand, taking that last step out into space together, not to plummet but to be held, held up in a mighty hand — it doesn't have to be God, it could be an energy force of some kind. That would do it, wouldn't it? Yes, up there in space she can see Susan in a pastel robe nodding in affirmation. And there's music, Beethoven, just the tag end of the "Missa solemnis," then the first few bars of Louie's own "Ain't Misbehavin'."

ACKNOWLEDGMENTS

Parts of this novella have appeared as stories, with some alteration, in the following journals: *Gargoyle,* "A Dog with Yesterday's Name"; *Alaska Quarterly Review,* "Minutes"; *The Sun,* "The Grand Boy"; and *The Summerset Review,* "Going to Granada with a Young Man."

Great thanks to many knowing friends for their editorial comments and to the late Judith Daniels for a professional grant.

Zane Kotker has published five novels: *Bodies in Motion, A Certain Man, White Rising, Try to Remember,* and *The Inner Sea.* Her short stories have appeared in a number of journals including the *Alaska Quarterly Review* and *The Antioch Review.* She's honored to have received a fiction grant from the National Endowment for the Arts and a couple of Pushcart nominations as well as to find her chapbook, *Old Ladies in the Locker Room and Pool,* a finalist for the 2012 poetry book award from the Massachusetts Center for the Book. She lives in western Massachusetts, where she can be reached through her website, zanekotker.com.